What readers are ;
Dance of the Jagua, .

I just finished reading your book. It was wonderful. I wanted it to go for another 200 pages. I could not put it down. It is a great book. How long before the second one? I bought a second copy for is a friend. I can't say enough good things.
—*Linda Budd*

I am so moved by the power the book has to remind me, truly and deeply, of who it is I truly am. I am so excited to share this book with everyone I care about.
—*Dana Anderson*

The book was absolutely perfect. I couldn't put it down, and I read half the night, even though I had a big business proposal to do for the next day.
—*Bernadette Williams*

Your book was wonderful. I am anxious for a sequel. Please say that there will be one. My friend Bill and I enjoyed reading it to one another. It was so much fun to discuss.
—*Claire Enloe*

I love your school for the lost arts. Is any of your book true? If it is, then you will have to share your secrets. This is a fantastic adventure story with lovely bits of wisdom—a totally satisfying read.
—*June Owen*

I just finished your book!!! It was fantastic!!! Muchas gracias for that ending. I loved the cat shapeshifting and being impatient. And I liked the neighbor, Carol, always being negative. I also like the

ancient wisdom school. I totally enjoyed every page of the book!!!
—*Laurie Van Vliet*

Girlfriend....I just finished reading your wonderful first novel. It was amazing. How did you get so wise? OK, I'm ready for the next one.
—*Tamara bearheart West*

This is like Harry Potter for women! Loved it!
—*Kathie Hightower*

I loved *Dance of the Jaguar*. I know that it is one book that I will be rereading many times. Martha's journey is fascinating, and the messages contained within the story are life changing. I highly recommend it, especially to women's readers groups.
—*Paige Lovitt, Reader Views*

TERRY

Dance of the
Jaguar

ANDREWS

Note for Librarians: A cataloguing record for this book is available from Library and Archives
Canada at www.collectionscanada.ca/amicus/index-e.html
ISBN 1-4120-9734-7

Printed in Victoria, BC, Canada. Printed on paper with minimum 30% recycled fibre.
Trafford's print shop runs on "green energy" from solar, wind and other environmentally-friendly power sources.

Offices in Canada, USA, Ireland and UK

Book sales for North America and international:
Trafford Publishing, 6E–2333 Government St.,
Victoria, BC V8T 4P4 CANADA
phone 250 383 6864 (toll-free 1 888 232 4444)
fax 250 383 6804; email to orders@trafford.com
Book sales in Europe:
Trafford Publishing (UK) Limited, 9 Park End Street, 2nd Floor
Oxford, UK OX1 1HH UNITED KINGDOM
phone +44 (0)1865 722 113 (local rate 0845 230 9601)
facsimile +44 (0)1865 722 868; info.uk@trafford.com
Order online at:
trafford.com/06-1490

10 9 8 7 6 5

Acknowledgments

It is possible for life to be as big and glorious as we can dream. To my many teachers on this path, thank you. Painting my life, stroke by stroke, has taught me that happiness begins with knowing myself.

Thank you from my heart to those who were generous with their time and love: My son, Amadeo Lasansky, for reading the manuscript on your vacation and designing a bold, beautiful cover. My brother, Steve Andrews, for successfully trying some of the techniques. My parents, for never stopping me from writing. Roger Masse, Patrick Kelley, and Shirley Baca, my audience for the first reading, and Patrick, for editing the final draft. Tim Reed, a contemporary buddha, for believing in the journey. Peg Geery, for your support and endless enthusiasm. Anne McCambridge, for your friendship and inspiration. Kathleen Liebenow, for you. Katy Young, for your energy-perfect beach house gatherings. Jill O'Carroll, for helping me to see another world. Kari Valente, for loving books. Peter Hughes, who promised to buy this book, sight unseen. And Katey Walters, who always brought me feathers.

To the hummingbird who led me to the nagual, thank you. To my cat, who joined me in the dance of transformation late one night, thank you. To the wizard who brought in healing energies from another realm, thank you.

And to you the reader, thank you. The adventure is the journey to wholeness, happiness, and fruition.

1

On the first day of spring, Martha Peggity was buying flowers at the farmer's market when she felt a pebble in her shoe. Spying an empty folding chair nearby, she cut through the throng of shoppers to sit down. "Now what?" her friend Liz asked, studying some watercolors at the next booth.

At the same moment, a half continent away, a feathered serpent formed in the shadows and prepared to descend a pyramid. A crowd had collected, among them a professor, his video camera in hand. He took a drink from his bottle of tepid water and then jostled in the humid heat for a better position.

Deep in a rainforest adjacent to the archaeological site, Aurora Luna sat in serene silence on a meditation cushion, her eyes closed. Knowing that the serpent would soon begin to move, she waited for a message. It was a moment of alignment and convergence not seen on the planet for some time.

Shaking her shoe out, Martha apologized to the card reader for using her chair. The woman's dark eyes took her in. Her auburn hair, accented by aquamarine earrings, gleamed. "What is your question?" Her long fingers shuffled a deck of cards.

Taken aback, Martha consulted her friend Liz, who giggled nervously and asked, Why not? A sense of obligation for using the chair propelled Martha forward. This was a new experience, but maybe Liz was right. What harm could it do? Maybe she could ask about the house.

"Would you like some guidance?" Martha nodded and the reader directed her to focus on her question as she shuffled the deck. Martha wondered if the potential answer was really taking shape in the cards, which looked too worn to hold anyone's destiny. The reader lowered her eyes. Moving her hands over the cards, she spoke quietly, asking for direction. As she did so, the noise of the market seemed to fade. Martha's reluctance gave way to anticipation; she felt suspended in time, as if her past had vanished and her future had not yet been dreamed. Oddly magnetized by the uncertainty, she waited.

Near the pyramid, the professor had found a good vantage point for taping. He had witnessed the event a few years earlier, but that was before he realized its significance. He wished the crowd would stop shifting. The aimless milling and noise distracted him. He wanted silence. *Tourists*, he thought. *They don't even know what they're watching.*

Deep in meditation, Aurora Luna lost her sense of time and place. Her breathing slowed until it was almost imperceptible. In her relaxation, she no longer felt her body. She merged with a universal heartbeat that sustained her. In this state, she was open to perceiving energy, particularly energy that had not manifested in a physical form. This was how she would receive a message if it came.

A breeze rattled the canvas canopy of the market stall as the reader turned the first card, which read *Death*. Looking at it, Martha felt a sense of dread. The woman studied her as if she didn't know where to begin. Martha thought, *I'm a goner.*

Her decision to go to the market, the pebble in her shoe, the empty chair: a seemingly random sequence of events had brought her face to face with a fortune-telling stranger. Why did things like this happen to her? She braced herself. In a few minutes it would all be over and she could go home, make dinner, and go about her routine for as long as she had left to live.

"In the same way that a seed falls to the ground and, given the right conditions, takes root," the reader began, "a seemingly random event can occur in someone's life and open new ways of seeing the world. It's part of the mystery, but this is how things happen." The reader tapped the Death card. "This shows a powerful new beginning, a second chance to live your dream. Something old gives way to something new. A part of you that you no longer need will die."

Martha recoiled like a fish that had just been hooked. Liz leaned closer.

"Would you like another card?"

What choice did she have? She bent over the table to gain some privacy, wanting details, as the serpent began its slow descent. It was a form that wasn't a form, only the appearance of one: a shadowy representation of an ancient, unfulfilled legend. There was little explanation of what it meant, like a riddle with no answer. Yet there had to be an answer, the professor thought as he recorded; the pyramidal puzzle must lie in its ritual with the sun.

Aurora felt the stirrings of movement, the representational transition. An open channel, she waited. She had done this before. When the message came, if it came, she was ready. She had spent two weeks in the Cloud Forest House preparing, quieting her mind, consulting her charts.

The reader turned another card. After a few seconds, which seemed like an eternity, she said, "You are standing in a doorway of opportunity. You are crossing a bridge to a bigger life. You will be traveling and learning new things. You have many abilities that are untapped. It is important to begin to focus on yourself. It seems you have always put yourself last."

Martha tried to anchor these statements to her daily reality. She did have a trip planned. Who didn't? And of course she had put herself last. That's what women did. They took care of everyone else. What did this mean? Should she take a painting class? What kind of opportunity? How would she recognize it?

There was an audible gasp from the crowd as the head of the serpent in front of the pyramid seemed to move. For the professor it was an electric moment. It was stone, how could it move? But he was certain it did. "*Mira!*" cried a small boy on his father's shoulders, pointing. What were they looking at? He squinted as the setting sun glinted off something metallic.

"Something unusual will happen." The reader pointed at the next card, flashing a large silver ring. Martha felt something brush against her leg. Her bag had toppled over, spilling kettle corn. A yellow lab trotted over to investigate. "Hank, no!" The sturdy dog gulped the treat. Martha grabbed the bag to right it as the owner retrieved the dog. "This is a very important card. It signifies responsibility and power. Remember your power."

Martha studied the card, which showed a lovely woman in a filmy gown floating in a magical garden, but it meant nothing to her. Liz butted in. "The suspense is killing me. What's going to happen? Give us some facts."

The reader shushed her with a finger to her lip, but Liz had put words to Martha's concerns. Suddenly she felt worried. What had she started? Liz, growing impatient, drummed her fingers on her leg as the reader, whose dark eyes had grown even darker, moved to the last card.

In the slanting sun, the diamond-backed serpent continued to move. In a few minutes it would be gone. With his videotape, the professor hoped to find answers he had long sought, answers that would help him unravel the riddles he had spent his career investigating. The myth that had grown up around the serpent had possessed him. He wanted to penetrate the mystery. Back in his office, he would be able to study the tape for telltale clues.

Aurora watched the serpent's descent on an inner screen that only she saw. She knew time was running out. If there wasn't a message soon, the information would be lost, and with it, the vision she had held for so long. If it disappeared wordlessly again she…she stopped herself, remembering her years of training. Once again, she quieted her mind and waited, trusting in the power of the ancients to reestablish the connection.

"The next step," the reader said suddenly, "is up to you. But I'm not sure you have a choice. It appears to be your calling." She paused, and Martha sensed that she was trying to emphasize the message so that it would be understood. "It is important to follow your heart. Let your inner wisdom be your guide, whatever happens." She collected the cards as Martha, not as enlightened as she hoped, paid.

"Talk about throwing money away," Liz snorted as they left. "What a bunch of baloney. Some soothsayer she is."

"It was your idea." Martha was miffed with Liz for having pushed her to do the reading, which had created more questions than it answered.

"It was not my idea. You sat in the chair. All I said was, why not."

"Next time *you* do it. See if she gives you any facts."

Liz sighed. "I thought they were supposed to tell you you're going to meet a tall, handsome stranger who still has his own teeth." She opened the trunk of the car to put her bags in. "So what do you think she meant? Does any of it make sense?"

"Don't I wish." Martha climbed in the car. "But if some part of me that I don't need is going to die, let it be my forgetfulness."

In front of the pyramid the ground rattled. Henry heard shouts and screams. As the crowd began to surge in his direction, he looked for an escape. He pressed his slender frame toward the exit, keeping his center of gravity low. The molten crowd seemed impenetrable. Worried that it was out of control, he ducked into a doorway and made his way down a narrow hall into a room so black he had to grope his way. A startled iguana skittered by, making his heart pound. He pressed against the wall, wishing he'd brought a flashlight. The musty smell was oppressive. He waited, listening to the pandemonium outside. And then the ground shook again, an unmistakable earthquake. Fear gripped him. Staring into the disorienting darkness, he held his breath to listen, wondering if he would be buried alive by the massive rocks. All at once a soundless shaft of light penetrated from above, and across the room, a pair of green eyes gleamed.

The feathered serpent looked directly at Aurora. It seemed to breathe fire; she could feel the heat. The eyes flashed. Thunder reverberated. But it wasn't thunder; it was a seismic voice that shook the ground. The words in the ancient tongue deafened her, and for the first time in ages, Aurora felt the prickle of fear on her skin. She fought it, needing to stay focused. From the depths of her being she summoned every ounce of energy, calling on her power to stand with her now. The serpent roared with a force that rocked the cosmos. I…AM…QUETZALCOATL. It hit her like a tidal wave, knocking her senseless, so that she didn't hear the rest. THE ONE…WHO RETURNS…NOT ONLY…IN SHADOW.

On the drive home, Martha thought about the reading while Liz babbled about nothing. Occasionally she said "Hmm," but her mind was elsewhere. Lately she'd been feeling that there had to be more to life, but she didn't know what. It was a vague restlessness that she couldn't pin down. Maybe she hadn't challenged herself enough. After Liz dropped her off, she made her way up the walk to her two-story colonial, unlocked her door, and went in. As she put away her purchases, the words repeated in her mind: *Something unusual will happen.*

Impulsively she grabbed her car keys. Moments later she was high on Owl Hill, parked outside a comfortable-looking Cape Cod. She had noticed in the paper it was for sale, and for some reason she felt drawn to it. It needed some work, and she hadn't looked at it because she knew her son would be opposed to the idea. But because of her reading she stepped out of the car and went up the walk. It wouldn't hurt to look around, maybe peak in the windows and stand on the porch to admire the view. And what if she did decide to buy it? She'd always wanted a house like this. Her heart skipped a beat as she considered such a rash idea.

A car pulled up outside as she looked around. A man climbed out and asked if he could help her, introducing himself as the agent handling the sale. "You'll have to act fast if you're interested," he told her. "I've got a buyer ready." He let her in, and she looked around. Judging from the dust, the house had been vacant for some time. It sorely needed updating: the carpet was vintage, the wallpaper ancient. "It needs some TLC," the agent agreed, "but it's structurally sound." His cell phone rang, and he stepped outside to take the call.

Walking through the house, Martha began to rethink her idea, but off the kitchen she found a den, painted the color of a tropical sunset. For some reason, a picture came into her head of a trip she had always wanted to take: a hotel in the heart of Mexico, margaritas on the terrace, bougainvillea thick on the wrought iron rail above the pool. It was odd to think of that now.

On the wall was a carved wood mask, apparently a piece of folk art. Its glass eyes gleamed with uncanny aliveness. A leather tongue hung from an open mouth as if the creature had just chased down prey, and its fangs were at the ready. The mask was realistically painted yellow with brown spots. As she carefully lifted it from the wall, an old handwritten tag dropped out—El Tigre, 1937, it read, Dance of the Jaguar.

Something made her put it on. Peering through the mouth, she began to move with languid steps. *Remember your power.* A low growl rumbled in her throat. She heard the agent returning, his shoes scudding in the hall. I'll buy the house, she thought, making up her mind at that instant. Suddenly she felt as if she had been set free from a lifetime of living for others. There was a swirl of air, and she turned to see if the window was open. The floor seemed to give way beneath her but she had no sense of falling. She also had no sense of fear, when, without a sound, the house she had been standing in disappeared.

On the plane home, the professor fell into a restless sleep. For a few minutes he dreamed; he was standing at the edge of the pyramid when a serpent rose out of the shadows, looming larger and larger, until its shadow covered the crowd. And then, without warning, it struck. The strike was like a lightning bolt, unexpected and illuminating everything in its path. He awoke with a start to the drone of the engines and the flight attendant taking his empty glass. "Are you alright, sir?" He nodded, but it was several minutes before his heart stopped thudding in his chest.

When Aurora opened her eyes, she was on the floor. Nothing appeared to be amiss, and she was exhausted but unhurt. She made some yerba maté to revive her body and spirit, sprinkling orange peel into it. The feathered serpent had appeared, big as life. And he had spoken, naming himself. That much she knew. But the rest was a jumble. All these years she had attempted to make the connection. Now she had, but having only legend to go on, she had misjudged the possibility. She needed to talk with Olivia.

2

Birds called from the dense overhead canopy, and monkeys screeched nearby. The air was thick with the honeyed fragrance of flowers. A brilliant blue butterfly drifted by as Martha, feeling firm ground beneath her feet, took off the mask and looked around to get her bearings. "I must be dreaming," she said with disbelief. She was in the midst of a jungle, where everything around her competed for space and light. Staring at a remarkable orchid, she tried to make sense of what had just happened.

No one, she realized, knew where she was. Now what?

Something slithered across her foot and she jumped to the side with a scream. If only she could call for help…. But her cell phone was in her purse, which was in her car in front of the Cape Cod. Her head was spinning. If only her son were here. Clark taught anthropology at the college and would maybe know where they were. He was an avid hiker and she wished now she'd gone to his talk at the gradeschool on wilderness skills last week instead of getting a pedicure and a facial. An animal rooted in the brush, giving her the willies. What if it came out? It was time to act. Wishful thinking was time wasted.

She needed a plan. All she had with her were her car keys, a little bit of change, and the mask. After checking carefully for spiders and snakes, she sat down on a nearby log by some huge ferns. Her best course of action might be to stay put because she didn't have a machete to hack a path through the vines. At least there were no lions and tigers and bears—yet. But what would the night bring?

As she studied a line of leafcutter ants, she heard a sharp cry. It came from a tree off to the left. She peered into the branches and presently spotted an iridescent bird that seemed to change color before her eyes—first red and royal blue, then emerald and gold. She wished she had her camera. The large bird eyed her intently, and she stood up to get a better look, moving slowly so as not to scare it.

She was unprepared when it swooped down on her. She ducked and ran, but the vines grabbed at her like guards. The bird was so close she could feel its talons just above her head. The jungle seemed to close in on her as she pushed through the dense foliage, until she could barely breathe. She stumbled, then fell. Lying on the ground, there was nothing left to do but cover her head and scream into the dirt.

As promised, Clark stopped by his mother's house on his way home from the college. There was no sign of life when he rang the bell so he let himself in. After checking the garage and finding the car gone, he realized she was out. Odd, when she was expecting him. She must have forgotten. Either that or something more interesting came up. He was glad she had gone out. Lately, she didn't seem to be doing that much because she was tired. It worried him. She was fifty-five and he wondered how soon he'd have to start taking care of her. He had his own family to look after and his two children were a handful. He changed the lightbulb in the kitchen and looked at a piece of notebook paper on the counter on which his mother had put two headings: Untapped Abilities and What I Still Want to Learn. Under the first column she had written "painting?" and under the second "Spanish, tai chi, and ceramics." Evidently she was planning to take some classes. She must have seen something on television about expanding her horizons. He felt happy about that. The newspaper on the table was open to the real estate section, and he glanced at it, wondering if she was finally thinking about moving to a condo. He liked the family home and was reluctant to part with it. Still, there was maintenance every year, and he was always fixing something for her. A condo would free him up from that.

Liz called twice and got no answer. She wondered what Martha was up to. Maybe she'd gone to see her grandchildren. Liz had checked the Internet for information on tarot cards and found a site that suggested you teach yourself. She wanted to tell Martha not to put too much stock in what she'd heard at the market. Martha was her oldest friend; they'd known each other since high school. She knew Martha would go home and worry over what the reader said.

At the Cloud Forest House, Aurora Luna was putting things away. She would leave shortly to return to Cuernavaca. As she thought about the feathered serpent's visit, she realized that interpreting his words would be easier if she had the book. But it had been mysteriously taken from her library several years ago and never returned. It worried her, someone else having it. But no one she knew had the power to use the information in it, yet. Time was of the essence now. She would have to improvise. As she looked through the plants she had gathered, including ca cal tun and cha-cha, she noticed there was one she had failed to find. She had a few minutes left and went quickly out, remembering she had seen some to the west. She imagined that Olivia and Steven were starting dinner. She missed them both. It was difficult to be away for so long.

After a few moments, when nothing happened, Martha cautiously got up. There was no sign of the bird, save for one long, luminous green feather. She brushed off her clothes and finger-combed her hair. She had lost the mask, but she couldn't waste time looking for it in the fading light. It would be dark soon. She plucked the feather from the ground and quickly decided to walk in the direction it was pointing. Almost immediately she discovered a path, which went over a rise and down a hill. She walked for some time, growing thirsty. Presently the jungle opened on a clearing, and she squinted in the unexpected glare of the setting sun. Not far away stood a small hut. Hoping to find someone there, she moved toward it.

The door opened as she raised her hand to knock. A woman with a cloud of white hair motioned to her to come in and sit down. It felt good to rest. There was tea tasting of citrus and the drink revived her.

"I've never been so glad to see someone," Martha said, surveying the collection of unfamiliar herbs on the table. "Do you speak English?"

"Yes." The woman was polite but matter of fact. "Would you like something to eat?" She produced some warm empanadas, and Martha ate hungrily. "Are you visiting the pyramids?" Martha, unsure where to begin, hesitated, and the woman kept talking. "There's a site not far from here. Every now and then somebody strays from their tour group and ends up here."

Martha decided to take advantage of this ruse. "Yes. Perhaps you can point me in the right direction to go back."

But the woman studied her. "What pyramid is it?"

Martha had no idea, and she finally admitted as much. All at once she was afraid she might break into tears. She was exhausted, and she wanted nothing more than to go home. "Do you have a telephone?"

"No telephone, no electricity." The woman lit some candles. "You don't look like anyone I would have expected," she finally said, studying the feather stuck in Martha's shirt pocket. The woman asked if she could see it. "Where did you get this?"

Martha explained she had found it.

"Do you know what this is?"

Martha shook her head, saying only that it was from a beautiful bird.

"You saw it?"

Since the woman seemed interested Martha told her what happened. "It attacked me," she explained. "It gave me a pretty good scare."

"I see." The woman got a knife and a cutting board. Her movements were fluid and effortless; Martha had never seen anyone move in that way. "You probably don't have much experience with animals, especially animals in this part of the world," the woman said, slicing a mango. After Martha acknowledged she was right, she continued. "I'd like to tell you a story. This feather is from the quetzal bird. It is very valuable, and you must keep it safe. For the time being, you must tell no one you have it." Her tone was serious, and Martha, who was used to acquiescing, nodded. "The quetzal is a bird of wisdom and power, a symbol of life and abundance. It is almost extinct and rarely seen nowadays. It lives high in the mountains." She paused, letting Martha absorb her words. "There's time to learn more later. For now, it's enough to know that you were given this gift for a reason."

Martha set her cup down and drew back. "I'm not sure what's going on," she said, "but I'm a long way from home. I suspect this is all a misunderstanding. If I give you the feather, will you tell me how to get back?"

A large orange cat materialized, jumped into a chair across from her, and eyed her intently. "That's Chaco," the woman said. "I'm Aurora Luna. You'll be seeing a lot of us." She looked at Martha expectantly. "And you are—?"

Martha introduced herself. "But I can't stay," she said. "I am in the middle of buying a house. Or I was…." Her voice trailed off as she thought about what had happened. She didn't like the way the cat was staring, and because of her unsettling experience with the bird she shifted uncomfortably in her chair.

"You don't like cats either?" Aurora asked.

"I don't know much about them," Martha replied. "Will he jump at me?"

When Aurora assured her that he wouldn't, Martha took a deep breath and let her eyes take in the modest room. "This is my home away from home," Aurora said, following her gaze. "It's small but it serves its purpose. I didn't realize you'd come here."

Martha did a noticeable double take. "You sound as if you were expecting me."

"The first time can be challenging. You did very well."

"The first time?" Martha didn't like the sound of that.

Before Martha could ask where she was, Aurora answered. "Central America."

Martha shook her head. "How is that possible? I live in Oregon."

"Then I'd be more careful if I were you." Aurora laughed and poured more tea. "These portals go everywhere."

The more Martha heard, the less she understood, but Aurora's voice had a calming effect on her, and the expressive eyes seemed to see to the center of her being. "You're here because you opened a portal that has been dormant for years. A portal," she continued, anticipating the question, "is a metaphysical door, a connection to other places and dimensions. A portal creates immediate access to somewhere else. It's a very useful tool." Aurora spoke quietly with no apparent emotion; her manner was serene. Yet as attentively as Martha listened, the explanation eluded her.

"How do I open it so I can go back home, and then seal it so I never fall through again?" she asked.

Aurora's eyes were so penetrating that Martha grew quiet. "Once you have the power to open a portal there are certain things you need to know."

"I'm sure it was an accident," Martha offered. She wondered if she should mention the mask, and then all at once the words were out of her mouth about having lost it.

Aurora removed an amulet from around her neck and Martha fell silent again. "You have chosen to follow a risky but necessary path. That is why the quetzal spoke to you."

"This is very different from anything I have ever experienced," Martha said. "I hope you can understand why I am having trouble with this whole idea."

Aurora poured more tea, and the aromatic fragrance enveloped them. "Celestial Citrus. We call it the drink of the gods. It will give you mental clarity and a sense of vitality because it's chockful of vitamins and antioxidants. I gathered the leaves myself. Now, we might as well get down to business. We have a few things to go over."

Mystified, Martha felt like she was back in high school chemistry and the explanations were just beyond her comprehension. Aurora pushed the amulet toward her. "As I said, you have opened a portal that was out of use for a long time. Only certain people have the power to do this. That power is both a responsibility, to be taken seriously, and a gift, to be enjoyed." She paused to let the words sink in.

"I'm afraid you've lost me," said Martha, struggling to keep up. At that moment the cat padded out of the room, distracting her.

"It's a lot to hear all at once. You might prefer to take the class. We stress hands-on practice."

"I can't stay." Martha was alarmed. "I didn't tell anyone I was leaving."

"When you change your mind, let me know. With a little notice, we can arrange everything for you."

Martha was reluctant to ask, but since she wanted to be on her way home soon she did. "What is it that I need to know?"

"I'll give you the condensed version," Aurora said. "Listen carefully. You don't need to write it down." She sat very straight in her chair, and her words floated into Martha's awareness like the notes of a sweet melody played by a flute. "There is a gossamer veil between the worlds that blows open for some of us, allowing us to see the interconnection between all things. Experiencing the interconnection brings us into harmonious interaction, and harmonious interaction carries us into cocreation. This is the responsibility. Here is the gift. Everything you need you already have, and it will arise as you need it. Every action is connected to the whole, and intent is the impetus of action. Emotion is a guide, intuition is a tool."

As the woman continued Martha felt her mind go blank. It was as if she was listening from a deeper place. Something in the recesses of her psyche was being stirred by an elemental force. She felt an unexplained quickening, and her unanswered questions evaporated. The woman's voice was like a song. Sometimes Martha felt she was hearing the melody, other times the words.

"You will discover the rules you live by don't work," the woman was saying. "The things you believe in don't exist." The aroma of the tea was as sweet as her voice. "You will give up the need to control, and you will create what you need. The moment of creation will be effortless, as in a dream." Martha felt like she might float away at any minute. "You will live simply, and lack nothing. Chaos will give way to inner calm; resistance will become irresistibility." The woman held out the amulet. "You need to trust one person especially—yourself. Because the realm of possibility is limitless."

Martha reached for the jewel. At first it appeared to be a piece of clear quartz, but when she held it up to the light, it seemed to come alive, like a snow globe she had as a child. She was unprepared for the almost electric charge that shot through her as she put it around her neck. She felt incredibly alive. "From this moment," Aurora said, "your life will never be the same."

Martha wondered what she had started.

Aurora smiled. "You are still thinking in a passive way. You must learn to live with intention. I suggest you stay for the class and the hands-on practice."

Martha's cheeks flushed. She'd never been around anyone who knew what she was thinking. Perhaps if she explained her situation she could go home and pick up where she left off, as if the whole experience could be dealt with like a dropped stitch in knitting. "I'm quite ordinary," she said. "I am certainly not a trailblazer. My hobbies are gardening and baking." She prattled on out of nervousness, not realizing she wasn't saying anything of note. She grew quiet as the cat passed by again.

She talks too much. Send her back.

Aurora spoke to the cat in Spanish, then said, "Please continue."

Martha began to wonder if a few more details about her life would make any difference. "I love to read. I stayed home to raise my son, so I've never worked. Murray and I planned to travel, but he died unexpectedly." She looked at the woman for a response but got none, so she went on. "My life revolved around my husband and his career."

The woman studied her for a moment. "So his life was your life." Martha nodded. Finally, she was getting somewhere. "Yes," the woman said, "your culture teaches women to invest in men. The natural outcome is the loss of native abilities that are key to the process. The experience is counterintuitive." She began to bundle her herbs. "You must learn to invest in yourself. Otherwise your spiritual and emotional bank account will be empty. At the school you will learn to give from the overflow of a full cup. This is giving from abundance. You will find that giving this way revitalizes you."

It was more than Martha could take in. In fact, her mind gave up making sense of any of this. At that moment, in her psyche, something moved. It was like the shifting of the continental plates before an earthquake, releasing pressure. She relaxed. A giggle rose to the surface like a bubble. And then, like lava, spontaneous giggles spilled from her core, freed from somewhere deep inside. She couldn't stop. She kept on until tears streamed from her eyes.

"You can stay as long as you like, or you can go." The woman's voice was soothing. "Just remember, if you want something, be clear that you want it. Being wishy-washy is a waste of time."

Martha stifled the last few giggles and dried her eyes. Her confusion had given way to clarity. "I'm going home," she said in a voice so strong it was unfamiliar.

"One last thing," Aurora said.

But Martha left too quickly to hear. The feeling of comfort was enormous and she breathed a sigh of relief to discover she was back in the den of the Cape Cod. Her car was still outside, and she was almost home. She switched on a light and saw that the mask was still gone. She was sorry she'd lost it. As she made her way to the living room, she heard the front door open. Somebody else was in the house.

3

The police questioned Martha in the garden as the neighbor eyed the house from a safe distance. "Tell us how you got back in the house," one of the officers asked, seeking clarification. "Dean said it was locked up." He gestured at the agent, who was checking to make sure all the doors were locked.

Martha considered what to say. She wanted to be truthful, but how could she mention the portal?

"Ma'am?"

As she began to explain, her son appeared to see what was going on. "Is there a problem?" he asked the officers as he walked up and took charge.

"We got a call about a prowler. Apparently it was just your mother. The agent showed her the house a few hours ago."

Martha checked her watch and was surprised to see it was two in the morning. She didn't realize she'd been gone that long. Besides, she felt rejuvenated and full of energy, ready to take on the world. The officers took down her address and phone number for their report and then left, calling the incident a mix-up. Clark reached over and plucked a piece of vine from her sleeve. "You're usually in bed by now," he said. "What's going on?"

"I've been in Central America," she whispered, excited to share her news and beginning to feel more courageous now that she was back.

He studied the piece of vine before giving it a toss, then shook his head. "Are you taking a night class?" He decided she must be enrolled in something at the college, probably Spanish. But before she could answer his question, the agent, wearing slippers, his sweatshirt inside out, came over to apologize. "I'm terribly sorry," he said, looking bleary-eyed and stifling a yawn. "I didn't realize you were still in there."

"I want to make an offer," Martha replied. When Clark protested, she said that the matter wasn't up for discussion. The agent said they'd talk in the morning, and Clark followed her home to make sure she arrived safely. She put the quetzal feather in a vase on her shelf. It would be safe there for the time being. Then she fell into a sound sleep.

That night she dreamed she could fly. She felt alive and joyous. Far from home, she saw a city in the jungle. As she flew closer to investigate, a majestic bird stopped her. "Take this," it said, offering a stone carving and a small book. But the stone made her fall from the sky, so she dropped it. Grasping for it, she dropped the book as well.

She woke up flailing her arms. It was only five-thirty and still dark, but she was too unsettled to sleep. The images tugged at her as she made coffee. Extending her arms, she pretended to soar. The next thing she knew, she had tipped over her mug of coffee. She mopped it up, wondering *What are my untapped talents?* When the newspaper came, she flipped through it aimlessly. Lately, it seemed to be full of nothing but violence and bad news. She had gotten cold feet about buying the house, and she began to feel that somehow she had imagined the experience in the rainforest. She ate breakfast and began to work the crossword puzzle, but when a six-letter word for door turned out to be portal, she put it aside. The messages, it seemed, were everywhere. By eight o'clock she had begun to feel anxious, and she worried about what to tell the agent. The telephone loomed large on the counter, and as she stared at it, her doorbell rang, startling her.

"You're not really thinking of buying the house, I hope," Clark said, handing her a rolled-up sheet of paper. "From Matthew. He wants to be a pilot. He made it at school."

She invited him in for coffee. As he poured milk in a mug, she opened the drawing. Her seven-year-old grandson had created a bold crayon portrait of himself flying an airplane. At the bottom of the page the teacher had included a banner with a printed quotation, and Matthew had drawn a line to it so the plane was towing the banner: Who we become, what we make of ourselves, depends on what we do with our lives—JOHN DEWEY.

It was as if the early-twentieth-century philosopher had just stepped into the room and uttered the words. "What we do," she repeated. It made perfect sense, and as she thought about action as the key, a plan formed in her head like a pearl in an oyster. She had a chance right now to do something bigger with her life, bigger than what she had done so far. Her first step was simply to take action. Intuitively it felt right, that much she knew. And so she told Clark she did want to buy the house. "I've never done anything like that," she said, convincing herself as well. "It's what I'm giving myself for my birthday." But the house wasn't the gift, she knew. The gift was a new approach.

He nodded as if he was trying to understand. "It doesn't make sense, mom. This isn't like you." But she had already dialed the agent. *Don't lose your nerve,* she thought. It was challenging enough to overcome Clark's resistance without having to sail against her own. Her son continued being practical. "Think of the upkeep. A condo would be maintenance free. You could spend some time traveling. Maybe go to Mexico, use your Spanish."

"I don't speak Spanish," she reminded him.

"Not yet," he said, "but you're learning. Take a couple classes to challenge yourself. Maybe you have too much time on your hands."

She waved him away as the agent answered and they made arrangements to meet. She asked her son to come by later with the children.

"Actually, we were hoping you would watch the kids," he said. "Can I drop them off at five? Leslie and I are going out."

"Of course you can, but you'll have to start giving me more notice," she said, the vision of her evening in the faraway hut tantalizingly fresh. "Just in case."

"Sure," Clark said. "But you're always home. I didn't think it was a problem."

By four o'clock Martha's offer had been accepted and she was on cloud nine. She arranged for a work crew to paint and clean and then called Liz. "You've lost your mind because of a fortune teller," Liz said. "Well, good luck. I'm anxious to see the place."

She didn't mention the portal just yet knowing that Liz's traditional belief system would be overwhelmed. Besides, for all she knew it was a one-shot deal, some kind of cosmic fluke that would never be repeated no matter how much she might enjoy another cup of that revitalizing tea with Aurora Luna. After all, she had lost the mask that had taken her there. And she had no idea how to contact Aurora. But there would be other opportunities. And she would definitely find out what her untapped abilities were.

Clark brought the children over at five. Matthew ran in and put his backpack on the couch in the family room. "Grandma, look what I brought," he called as Melissa, who was five, went into the kitchen to see what her grandmother was doing. "We won't be too late," Clark said, following her. "But go ahead and put them to bed at the normal time. Umm, smells like meatloaf." Melissa climbed up on a chair to check the counters. "What's that you're wearing, mom?" Clark, who had gone on an architectural dig in Mexico as a college student and had long been interested in artifacts, reached out to touch the amulet, which she'd forgotten about. "It looks ancient. Is it a replica?"

As he studied it, she remembered what Aurora said, that the piece was passed from one keeper to the next, down the lineage through time. It was better if she kept the details to herself until she knew why she had it. She was told to keep it safe too, like the feather. "It looks like it should be in a museum," he finally said. "Where'd you say you got it?"

"Let's talk later, when you have some time. I'm sure the kids are hungry."

"I'm not eating yucky green beans," Melissa said.

"Where's Bob the Bear?" Martha had Melissa set a place for her favorite stuffed bear and put a cookie on a plate for him. "If he eats his dinner, he gets a cookie," she said.

"What if I eat mine?"

"You get a cookie too."

As it turned out, Melissa ate three green beans, some rice, and all her meatloaf. She was too full to eat a cookie, so Martha put it in a bag for her to take home. The children fell asleep at nine, Melissa on the couch and Matthew in his sleeping bag on the floor, where he had set up camp in front of the fireplace. Martha watched the dying embers and thought about her new house. She'd be in at the end of the week. There was a lot to do—the movers would be coming to pack everything and she needed to arrange for phone and utilities. Ordinarily she would have been overwhelmed, but she felt content and peaceful.

For one brief moment she hoped she wasn't making a mistake. The idea made her cold. She pulled an afghan around her as the cold changed to fear. How could she be so confident one minute, and so unsure the next? She was fretting about having acted too quickly when her son arrived. He made a cup of cocoa and sat down for a few minutes in the kitchen while she put away the dishes from the dishwasher. "You seem different somehow, mom. I can't put my finger on why, but you seem stronger," he said. "More vital. More alive."

"That's how I feel," she said. Once again, she vividly felt the sense of connection she had experienced in the rainforest. She turned to Clark, who was stirring a marshmallow in his cup. "I feel like I've missed out on trying new things in my life. I'd like to do that now."

"I think that's great," he said. "It just seemed kind of sudden, impulsive even."

"If I think about it too long, I'll lose my nerve," she said. "I'm going to trust my intuition. And I think it's a good thing, because last night I dreamed I could fly. I'm spreading my wings, so to speak."

He rinsed out his cup in the sink, and she suggested he leave the children for the night. "Come have breakfast with us in the morning."

Back in Cuernavaca, her home in central Mexico, Aurora Luna conferred with Olivia Paz about her experience in the Cloud Forest House as she unpacked her herbs. "It was not what I expected," she said, recounting what she could remember of the message she had gotten. "And then an unlikely person showed up, a woman with no experience whatsoever. I wondered if it was an accident." Olivia listened intently as Aurora gave her the details. "I'm not feeling enlightened about this," Aurora added. "I thought it would be obvious and clear."

Olivia thought for a moment before speaking. "We've had several students register for the next session," she said. "Steven was impressed by a couple of them. Maybe we need to be patient and not jump to conclusions. It might be that the opportunity for an opening that was created when the feathered serpent spoke pulled someone in by mistake. We're all new to this process, and we don't know how it will play out. I say we wait and see what happens."

There were preparations to make for classes, and both of them went off to make them. Aurora tried to find Chaco, who had returned with her, but he was nowhere to be seen.

Due to remodeling delays, it took two weeks for Martha to get moved to her new house. Liz came to help her put things away, and she was settled in before she knew it. With its new carpet and paint, the Cape Cod was charming. Even Clark thought so. "I guess it was a good idea," he conceded. "It's all on one floor and there's lots of space." They wandered out to the large backyard garden, which was bursting with spring buds. Behind the rhododendron, the snippet of jungle vine had taken root and was sending out its first leaf.

Matthew and Melissa went to explore. "Grandma, can we build a fort?" Matthew shouted.

"Just be careful," she said. "I haven't had a chance to look around." They disappeared into the woods that lined the back of the property.

"Glad this place has someone in it again," the neighbor called from across the hedge. "Do you raise birds?" Martha shook her head. "Saw an unusual bird in your backyard this morning. Thought it might be a pet." The neighbor's name was Joe McIntyre and his wife, Carol, told Martha to come have coffee as soon as she could.

Clark arranged her garden furniture while Martha went back in the house for a hat. The sun was out, and she hadn't put on any sunscreen. A deliveryman rang the doorbell and handed her a package.

She drew back in disbelief when she looked inside to find the mask.

You'll create what you need.

The phrase from the hut drifted into her consciousness like cottonseed riding the wind. It was looking to root, but the idea was so new, so foreign to her existing belief system, that she couldn't hold on. Tantalizing as the concept was, her old ideas were in the way. Feeling unnerved, she took the amulet off and tucked it in a drawer. It was too valuable to wear, especially after Clark's comment that it belonged in a museum. Besides, she couldn't have things showing up just because she thought about them. Her house would be full! She wondered who had sent the mask. There was no return address.

She went to hang it in the den, which had been freshly painted the sunset color and was now comfortable and cozy with her furniture. "Let me see that," Clark said, coming in. "A dance mask. I saw some of these in Mexico. Where did you get this?" She told him, but when he started to put it on she stopped him.

"El Tigre," he read. "That means jaguar. I'll look up the dance," he said. "See if I can learn anything just for fun." He seemed to come to life. "You know, that summer in Mexico was incredible. It was my first experience in another culture." He studied the mask, remarking about the details of the carving and painting. "Art definitely enlarges our experience," he said, shifting into his professorial stance. "Artists order and reorder meanings to create new connections. This mask, for instance, is full of meaning and symbolism, even though we don't understand it. The artist, in creating the work, strikes a balance between the making and the magic. At some point, the two elements come together and captivate us. Don't you wonder what magic this mask held?"

After Clark left with the children, Martha went back into the den. On her way in, she caught her reflection in the mirror. She looked younger than her years. She was trim, and her thick hair, short and stylishly cut, had just begun to silver. She wondered for a moment why she would be chosen for anything special, especially something she didn't understand. She felt ordinary. Nothing in her life had ever distinguished her. And as far as she knew, she had no unusual talents. Her hand moved to her neck, which felt strangely empty without the jewel. *Intent is the impetus of all action.*

Impulsively, she made a decision. She went to get the urn she had kept for three years and carried it outside. She spread the ashes in the garden, working them into the soil. "I'm releasing you," she said, her eyes welling with tears of both sadness and joy. "I'm opening myself up to life as an adventure." She took a deep breath and let it out, releasing the weight of an obligation. A breeze rustled the branches nearby. Murray was free, and so was she.

Later, she stood by the door as the sun went down over the distant hills. Lights came on in the valley. Venus appeared. Her adventure in the rainforest seemed a long time ago, like she had dreamed it. She wondered if the woman with the white hair was watching the stars. *Your life will never be the same.*

In the dusk, she sensed a presence. "Murray, if that's you, I went to Central America," she said, wanting to tell someone. "I used a portal. It was like something in a movie," she added. "I wish I knew what it all meant, but it boggles my mind." She felt expansive again, as if she was more herself than she had ever been.

As the stars popped out in the inky darkness, she fell into a reverie. There was a whole universe to know and all she'd seen until recently was a small part of it. She wished she could remember everything Aurora Luna had told her, because it seemed important. She pulled a sweater around her shoulders, reluctant to go inside. For the first time in a long time, that day she had felt truly alive.

The birdbath was empty, and she went to fill it with water. The watering can had been tipped over. As she reached for it, the lights went off next door, making her feel vulnerable in the darkness. The shadows seemed to move, so with one more glance at the stars, she headed inside.

From the edge of the shadows, a cat watched her intently, alert to every sound and movement. Its eyes were bright, and its orange fur gleamed even in the dark. The hour had come; it padded toward the house.

4

In his office, Henry Hocket transferred the videotape to his computer so that he could study it for clues. He watched it several times, lamenting the fact that he was missing the sequence at the end. He had mapped out significant details on a large photo on his wall. He had also charted the serpent's descent so that he could make notes about it. His office was cluttered with open books, diagrams, photographs, and notepads. He had devoted twenty years of summers and spare time to finding the secrets the pyramid held, ever since learning that ancient people had recorded their ideas about the mysteries of the universe there.

He looked at the notes he had scribbled on the airplane, retracing what he already knew. The pyramid was constructed with architectural and astronomical accuracy; the snake that rose up out of shadow and slithered down the steps as the sun waned was due to the precise measurements of those who built the structure. He knew that a whisper uttered at one end of the 500-foot-long ball court, where he had stood, could be clearly heard at the other end, despite the wind or the time of day. This phenomenon had been extensively studied, but how it was accomplished remained a mystery. That was the problem, he thought, there was too much mystery. Even though these ancients had mapped the heavens and developed a writing system, even though they had mastered mathematics and constructed cities from stone without benefit of the wheel or metal tools, even though they'd left a huge imprint on the face of the earth, little was known of what they had actually learned. He had explored their temples and palaces and observatories for years and still gained no ground. He would have given up, save for learning that descendents of these ancient people were still alive and well and practicing, and waiting for the promised return of their feathered serpent.

He pulled the worn book from his desk. Obtaining it was his moment of glory, and he was still working on the painstakingly slow translation. As far as he could tell it contained information of Quetzalcoatl's return, but so far all he had translated was a record of the historical story, which was available elsewhere. Quetzalcoatl was a legendary figure who arose during the Toltec period in Mexico. He came to represent art and science, agriculture and technology, as well as the less definable and more elusive powers of wizardry. He left one day, promising to return. Much revered, he was depicted as a plumed serpent, the feathers representing higher consciousness and the serpent, wisdom, power, and magic.

Martha stared at the mask. The morning sun was bright; she ought to do some gardening, she thought, glancing out the sliding glass door. But the mask was magnetic; its eyes seemed to watch her. She wondered if it still had its power. If she threw caution to the wind, would it take her to the tiny hut? She had connected there with some lost part of herself that she longed to feel again. She wanted the sensation of being vibrantly alive, yet at the same time she was afraid. There were so many unknowns. *You have chosen to follow a risky but necessary path.* Why was it risky? Impulsively she took the mask off the wall and put it on. She waited, but nothing happened. She moved this way and that. She growled. She even turned in a circle and jumped up and down.

¡Ay, caramba! the cat said, watching from the bushes. *This will be a challenge.*

But Martha was unaware of his presence. She was focused on what was wrong. Her mind jumped to the obvious conclusion: she had already lost her newly discovered ability. Perhaps what had happened to her was a mistake. She thought about the young California couple who had wanted to buy the house. Maybe this was supposed to be their experience. If only she hadn't been in such a rush to return home. She should have stayed for the class, just to see what it was like, while she had the chance. Sometimes chances didn't come around again.

In the late afternoon her grandchildren, full of excitement about the new house, came for dinner. Clark, who walked them over, gave them both a big hug and then left. Melissa had brought her teddy bear. "She won't go anywhere now without it," Matthew explained. "She thinks he talks."

"He does talk," Melissa said.

Martha winked at the bear and welcomed him, then asked who wanted to eat by candlelight. The children cheered and she lit the candles on the table. "Let's see, Bob can sit there. Melissa, you sit next to him in case he needs help." She had grilled chicken and cooked rice. The house felt good with children in it. That's probably what was missing from her life—the joyful energy of children—rather than some mystical mumbo-jumbo that might take her away from the familiar routine of home and family.

During dinner she said they could each start a garden in the back. "Goody!" Melissa said. "I want to plant pumpkins and marshmallows."

"Marshmallows come from the store," Matthew said, rolling his eyes. Melissa screwed her face up in a frown, but Martha averted tears by suggesting that Melissa draw a picture of what her garden would look like. She ran to get her drawing pad and crayons from her backpack. Matthew helped clear the table, and while Martha loaded the dishwasher, he ran through the house pretending to be in an airplane.

A few minutes later she heard Melissa shriek in terror and run from the den. She hurried to check on her and nearly collided with Matthew, who was following in hot pursuit. He roared at her, gripping the jaguar mask with both hands. For a moment Martha was immobilized, unable to even speak as her mind raced with the possibilities of what could happen. She tried to act, but she was so afraid that her movements had the frustrating leaden motion of a dream sequence. Finally she was able to speak and retrieve the mask. "That's not to play with," she cautioned, carefully hanging it up even though she was shaking. She took a deep breath. "It's a dance mask. A very old one."

"How does the dance go?" Matthew asked. She admitted she didn't know, but said his father was researching it. "You can ask him about it. Now please play quietly for five minutes while I make a phone call." She went out to the kitchen but had barely dialed Liz when they returned.

"Grandma, look." Matthew was carrying a large orange cat, which looked at her in a fearless way. "He was outside."

"That's exactly where he belongs," Martha said, telling Liz she had to hang up. She went to open the door, but the cat jumped into a chair and sat down.

"Can we keep it?" Melissa asked.

"I'm sure it has a home," she replied as it dawned on her that she had seen this cat before. The cat studied her, waiting for her to remember.

The hair on her scalp tingled. How had it gotten here?

"It doesn't have a collar," Matthew said.

Seeing the cat put Martha on edge, as if she didn't know what might happen next. For some reason, the cat had come to her house and was looking at her in much the same way as it had in the hut in the rainforest.

"Can we feed him?" Melissa asked.

"No. We don't want to encourage him to stay." Martha had never had a cat, and she knew little about their care. Besides, he already had a home. The cat continued to stare, his gaze unwavering.

The telephone rang, and Martha went to answer it. It was Liz, wanting to know if everything was OK. "You hung up so suddenly," she said. Martha briefly told her what was going on and promised to call her in the morning. She fixed the children some dessert, and they were eating when Clark and Leslie arrived a short time later. "Mom, Grandma has a new cat," Melissa said, taking a bite of her ice cream. "I'm going to grow a garden."

"That's wonderful," Leslie said, breezing in. "But don't talk with your mouth full. Matthew, sit up straight, please. No slouching at the table." Matthew straightened. "I hope they weren't any trouble," she said, turning to Martha.

Deciding not to mention the mask, Martha shook her head. "Would you like some ice cream?" Leslie didn't, but Clark did, and they stayed a few minutes while he polished off the pint of chocolate fudge. The children followed the cat back into the den. "I didn't think you liked cats, mom," Clark said, putting the bowls in the dishwasher.

"I don't mind it," she said. "But I think it just came to visit." That wasn't the whole truth; she felt the cat, because of the way it was looking at her, was trying to tell her something. She was also hoping it might be able to help her contact Aurora.

The children went to collect their things. As Melissa left, she tugged on Martha's sleeve. "Grandma, Chaco can fly."

"What, dear?" But before she could determine what Melissa meant, Leslie had scooped her up and carried her to the car. After they were gone Martha sat down in the den. The cat showed no signs of leaving.

She decided to consult him. "I wonder if you can tell me how I can visit Aurora again." She waited, but the cat said nothing. "I tried putting the mask on." The cat stared impassively. She tried to remember what his name was.

Chaco.

"That's right. Chaco," she said as the name popped into her head. "How can I contact Aurora?"

You should have kept the amulet on, for starters.

Suddenly she thought about the amulet and went to get it. It wasn't in the drawer although she was sure she'd put it there. She wracked her brain, trying to think where it was.

You can use the mask. I'll walk you through it.

She stared at the mask on the wall. It was late. She would wait until the morning, after breakfast. She'd get a good night's sleep and then go.

Martha was finishing breakfast when her phone rang. "Mom." Clark's tone was apologetic. "Matthew took your feather home because he wanted to take it to school. He's sorry he didn't ask, but that's not why I'm calling. A friend just stopped by and Matthew showed him the feather. He was very interested in knowing where you got it."

Martha, who was just going to call Clark to tell him she would be out for the day, glanced at the vase where the quetzal feather had been to find it empty. "Matthew should not have taken it," she said, dismay clumping in her throat. "It's important that he return it at once." She thought about her instructions to guard it carefully and wished now she had put it somewhere that was safer.

Clark assured her they'd get it back to her. Their friend had borrowed it and promised to return it. "He was wondering if he could meet you."

Martha was growing worried. "You really shouldn't have loaned it without asking. I'm feeling quite concerned about this," she said.

Clark, who could tell she was upset, promised to go get the feather and come by with it in a couple of hours.

Martha, meanwhile, put on some comfortable clothes and filled a fanny pack with a few essentials: a flashlight, an energy bar, lipstick, and a pen. She wondered about a passport. She didn't have one; she jotted it down on a list on her refrigerator. She planned to leave as soon as Clark brought the feather back, and her excitement was growing. The cat, evidently not interested in exerting any extra effort, watched from the back of the couch.

"I can't believe I'm feeling this eager," she said, somewhat surprised she was talking to a cat. "You'd think I knew what I was doing." She giggled. "What if I step into the portal and end up in the middle of Patagonia?"

The phone rang. This time it was Liz, wondering why she hadn't called. "I completely forgot," Martha said. "There's so much going on."

"Like what," Liz asked.

"The move, mainly," she replied. "Getting settled."

"Have you had anything unusual happen?"

The question caught her off guard, and Martha debated about how to answer. At some point, she thought, it would be fun to take Liz with her, but she was probably jumping the gun. So all she said was that Clark was coming by, and she needed to make some muffins.

But she had no intention of baking anything. She went out to the garden because the sun was bright, and while she was planning where to put the children's gardens, Carol called out a hello. "Listen, my brother's coming today. We wanted to invite you to dinner. I think you'd enjoy each other." She went on to say he'd lost his wife two years ago and needed cheering up. "We thought a change of scenery would be good, and we finally got him to agree to come. He's been so blue recently." Martha said she'd check her schedule, promising to call later. She checked her watch, wondering where Clark was, when he appeared with his friend in tow.

"There you are. We rang the bell." He introduced her to the professor, one of his colleagues at the university. He seemed reputable, and he had a warm handshake, but there was something about him that Martha didn't like.

"Tell me your name again?" she prompted, leading them inside.

"Henry Hocket," he replied. "I teach art history, but I'm a birdwatcher from way back. When Clark showed me the feather, I just had to find out more about it. I hope you don't find this intrusive, but I'd like to hear where you found it."

"Did you bring it with you?"

"I did," he said, producing a plastic case, "but I'm hoping you will let me keep it for a few days. I wanted to do some research about it." Suddenly Chaco appeared. His eyes became narrow slits, and his tail twitched back and forth, putting Martha on edge.

"Let me think about it. Could I give you a call?" Clark looked at her. His mother normally bent over backwards to help people, and he was surprised by this new turn in her behavior. Henry handed her his business card.

She told them she was on her way out but that she would be in touch. When they were gone, she pulled on her fanny pack and went to find Chaco in the den. But he had disappeared. Going into the living room, she noticed a woman coming up her walk wearing a wide-brimmed straw hat and sunglasses. She was tall and Martha was struck by how gracefully she moved. She was impeccably dressed in a crisp white shirt, black slacks, and sandals, and her heavy silver bracelet was inlaid with turquoise and obsidian. Martha wondered if she lived nearby. When Martha opened the door, the woman came in. She handed Martha a box, and the aromatic fragrance of Celestial Citrus surrounded them like a cloud. "I'm Olivia Paz," she said. "I teach with Aurora. Chaco told me you wanted to see her, but she was away today." Olivia settled into a chair as Martha prepared tea. "I hope I'll be able to help."

Martha felt her spine tingle. "I didn't know how to reach Aurora. I tried to use the portal...," she began.

"Trying is not the same as intending," Olivia said. "Intention is a willful act."

"Can you tell me how to do it, step by step?" Martha, confident that she wanted to try again—this time knowing what to expect—hoped for a formula.

"There isn't a formula," Olivia said patiently. "It's more intuitive than that. Think back to what you did."

"I put the mask on, and—"

"The mask isn't essential," Olivia said. "We'll try without."

Martha remembered thinking about Mexico, moving her hands, and growling.

"You won't need to growl either. Simply focus your energy, picture where you want to go, and *voila*! You're there. It's the only way to travel."

Momentarily taken aback, Martha lowered herself into a chair. "Do you mean I can go other places?"

"Once you master the technique, you can go anywhere." Seeing Martha's face light with interest, Olivia cautioned her, "You're a beginner. Beginners need practice. There's no sense ending up in Washington, D.C., if you're trying to go to Washington State. Or Hong Kong if you want London."

"Oh my," Martha said, "I've never been to any of those."

"Then maybe you won't mind ricocheting around."

Martha said she would prefer to know the technique. They sat quietly for a moment and all at once she thought about the amulet. As soon as she did, Olivia handed it to her.

"How did you—?"

"The moment you take it off it gets returned. That's what Aurora was trying to tell you when you left the Cloud Forest House so abruptly." Olivia chuckled. "I enjoy Level 1s, but they are so dramatic."

Martha frowned. "This is all very new to me, I'm afraid." She closed the gardening magazine she had left open on the table.

"As a Level 1 apprentice, you will need to be more disciplined. You'll never advance at the rate you're going. We'll be here all year before you master flying."

Martha felt her hair stand on end. Maybe this is why Aurora said *risky*. "What do you mean by flying?"

"You know, up in the air." Olivia flapped her arms.

"Like a bird?" Martha was unable to hide her shock. She stacked all her magazines in a pile.

"When you fly by intention, there's no need to actually move your arms. It's just that beginners sometimes do until they get the hang of it. That's how you can tell they're beginners. With Level 1s," she continued, now having Martha's full attention, "there's always a learning curve."

"Won't people see me? How high will I go? Why do I need to fly?" Martha fired questions like a corn popper gone amok.

"You're having trouble with the idea of intention. You've never used it." The woman was silent for a moment. "Don Chaco will help." She gazed in the direction of the doorway and Chaco padded in.

"Your cat?"

"He's not my cat. He's a Level 3. He comes and goes as he pleases."

"I fed him," Martha said. "I hope that was OK."

"Of course it was. He was a guest in your home."

Martha had grown as mystified as she was in the hut.

"It's best not to think too much. Align your thoughts and your actions and your words. Alignment intensifies the power. If you don't mind, I'd like to do some work with you. Please stand and close your eyes." Martha did as she was instructed.

Olivia started to circle her in a dance, moving this way and that. Martha began to feel odd sensations of energy moving through her. She felt very light, as if she were floating. "You may open your eyes," Olivia said. Her voice seemed to come from down below. "Remain relaxed. Remember to breathe. Let me do all the work."

When she realized she was floating, Martha gasped. "Breathe," Olivia instructed calmly. "That's good. Focus on breathing." Martha was bobbing around the room like a helium balloon, out of control. "You're turning. Good. A little more. You won't bob so much if you relax. Very good." It took a few minutes, but Martha finally realized she moved in the direction she thought about.

"You are beginning to experience your power," Olivia said. "You have always given it up to others. When you give it up, you compensate by needing to control. But controlling is not the same thing at all. There's no fulfillment from it. It's a hollow victory and a lonely experience."

Martha floated like the oversized butterfly in the rainforest. She felt an enormous sense of well-being, as if flying was a natural human endeavor. Where was the risk in this? Chaco eyed her from a distance. Then he jumped to the back of the couch for a better view. With another leap he was atop the armoire, at eye level. Distracted, Martha thought she was going to crash. "Don't think about it," Olivia said. "Think about landing gently. Left, more, more." She landed on the coffee table just as Olivia moved a vase of tulips. Safely down, Martha felt exhilarated.

"For now, practice indoors. It's good for going up and down stairs. As you get better at it, you'll be able to pick up speed. You'll find it's a very useful skill. Again, it's one of many." Olivia picked up her things to go. "I haven't had a Level 1 in some time." She handed Martha a business card. "When you're ready. Don Chaco, make sure she practices," she said, heading to the door. "She's going to need these skills shortly."

Martha looked at the card. The Ancient Wisdom School, it read, Cuernavaca, Mexico. There it was, the information she needed. "When I'm ready," she repeated. She decided to practice flying, just to see if she could do it on her own.

5

Henry Hocket was puzzled about Martha. Who was she and how did she obtain a quetzal feather? Certainly she didn't realize what it was. Her son had no idea and said he didn't think she had had it very long. Hocket tried to decide his best course of action. In an ideal world, she would give him the feather in the interest of science, due to its value and rarity. It was illegal to kill the birds because they were close to extinction, so it was difficult to come by an iridescent specimen that beautiful. He began to put together some information about the bird to give to her. Once she understood the situation, he hoped she would be more cooperative. He had photographed the feather with his digital camera, but he had not had a chance to try any of his experiments with it. It was one part of the answer, he felt, to the solution he was seeking.

After Olivia left, Martha decided to practice flying before she forgot the technique. She put away everything breakable and covered all the hard or sharp surfaces, like the brick fireplace hearth, with pillows.

Chaco watched her through the narrowed slits of his eyes, which missed nothing. He liked to occasionally upset the apple cart, knocking things off balance, as this was excellent preparation for unexpected events. It was fine and dandy to practice something indoors, in the safety of your house, for instance, but sooner or later you needed to be prepared to use your skills in the real world, navigating both the seen and the unseen dimensions. He wasn't sure if she had noticed his input or not, because humans saw what they wanted to see, but sooner or later she would. She was still caught in her own resistance, which limited what she could do. Her beliefs created the resistance. She didn't believe it was possible to fly. And because she was resisting, practice was crucial to progress. Once she understood the power of intention, practice would be unnecessary. He yawned. It was time-consuming. Humans thought cats had nothing better to do than sit and look out the window. He had a million better things to do but this was his assignment, and he knew he had to stay with it. Nobody would ask many questions about a cat hanging around.

On her first attempt, Martha lurched up a couple of feet and then dropped to the floor with a thud. "Ow," she said, going to get more pillows and strapping a set around her waist. On her second attempt, she managed to build up some speed and drift into the bedroom, where she knocked over a lamp. "This is crazy," she muttered.

¡Ay-yay-yay! I must be loco. Chaco walked to the center of the living room and leapt into the air. He flipped with acrobatic ease and then landed on top of the chair. *You're making it too hard. Just do that. Get the feel and practice control.*

"Easy for you," Martha said. "I suppose that's your idea of encouragement." But the next try seemed easier. Before she knew it an hour had gone by. She had banged into a few doorways, knocked a painting off the wall in the living room, and upended the arrangement of flowers and candles on the dining room table. But overall she felt good about her progress. Just before she quit her foot caught a small bowl of candy on the coffee table and scattered it over the floor. Chaco was relieved when she took a breather to get the mail.

As Martha stepped outside, a car pulled in next door and honked. Carol and Joe had just picked up Carol's brother at the airport. Joe swung a suitcase out of the trunk as Carol made the introductions. Ned Pine was friendly but quiet, Martha thought, although perhaps he was more talkative without his chatterbox sister around.

"Are you free for dinner tonight?" Carol asked. "We thought we'd go to the Inn on the River." Martha accepted, but that meant she had to put off trying to use the portal again. She headed back inside, not realizing Carol was behind her. "I was thinking.... Oh—." She stopped, surprised by the disarray of Martha's living room. "What happened?" she asked, picking her way over the candy on the floor.

"I was practicing my flying." Martha laughed as if she were making a joke. She was still feeling very light on her feet, and she took hold of the arm of a chair to steady herself.

Carol laughed too. "That's a good one. Flying. I like that. You'll have to teach me how you do it." Martha smiled politely.

They had a six-thirty reservation. Martha rummaged through her closet in search of a suitable outfit, but couldn't concentrate. She was thinking about what she had done. Despite the fact that it seemed impossible, she had flown! Who would believe that? She wished she could tell Liz. Finally, she pushed the flying lesson out of her head and settled on some slacks and a top. She grabbed a lightweight sweater in case they sat outside.

They pulled into the Inn on the River parking lot at six twenty-five. "Careful where you park," Carol instructed Joe. "I don't want some dimwit dinging the door."

"You can't control all the dimwits in the world," Joe said, "even if you want to, because some of them are smart enough not to listen to you."

Ned tried to ignore them. "How is the food here?" he asked.

"We like it," Carol said. "It's the best place in town. I imagine in the city you have more choices, so you may not care for it."

Martha sensed it was going to be a long evening.

Because it was warm, they decided to sit on the deck overlooking the river. "Pretty spot," Ned said, holding her chair. They placed their orders and chatted about the inn's history, which was written up on the back of the menu. After their food came Ned began to tell Martha about himself. He was a retired mechanical engineer and lived in St. Paul, Minnesota, near the Mississippi River. The river was a flyway for migrating birds, so he got in a lot of good bird watching close to home. "I imagine you see some interesting birds out here," he said to prompt an answer from her.

At the mention of birds, Martha felt an unmistakable sensation of lightness. Her cheeks flushed at the possibility that she might lift off in front of the other diners. She gripped her plastic chair as Ned began to discuss the aerodynamics of flight. Fighting to stay put, she contemplated her razor clams, which were getting cold, but her chair lifted off the deck. To make matters worse, a seagull wheeled overhead. Ned, leaning back to look at it, said he'd like to be a bird for one day so he could fly like that. Anchoring her arms securely under the table, Martha almost toppled Carol's water glass.

"Oh!" Carol reached for it. "This table's not very steady."

"Is your dinner OK?" Ned asked.

"Delicious." Martha noticed she was an inch or two higher than Ned.

"You're not eating."

"Perhaps I'll get a doggy bag." She wondered how much longer she could hold on.

"You give the rest of us a bad name," Carol said. "I was taught to clean my plate."

"Weren't we all," Martha replied, wanting to shift the conversation to a new topic. "You must be happy to have your brother visit, Carol."

"It's been ages," she said. "But I hope his mood improves."

"Wait till we play some golf," Joe said to Ned. "You'll feel like a new man."

Martha tightened her grip on the table once more. The ice in their glasses tinkled like bells. She fought a growing desire to simply let go. In a few minutes she'd be a speck in the sky, and in a few years, maybe they'd forget about how she floated off.

Joe decided to order dessert. He debated between the strawberry shortcake and a slice of pecan pie. "You don't need the calories," Carol said.

"Sounds like you want part of it," Joe retorted. "You don't like to share yours, but you sure want to share mine."

"Otherwise you'd be as big as a barn. It's for your own good."

Martha let go of the table and took Ned's arm, suggesting a walk. He was eager to oblige. A walking path followed the river, and lights had come on to illuminate it. Martha held on to Ned as her feet danced along the sidewalk like leaves in the wind. He pointed out a blue heron lifting off a little ways from them, and they watched the heron's great wings ply the air. "It doesn't seem possible, does it?" he said. "They give a jump and off they go." They had rounded a curve in the path, and the restaurant was no longer visible. Ned extended his arm. "I would die happy if I had a chance to fly."

That did it. Martha, no longer able to resist the impulse inside her, instructed Ned to jump and then hang on. "What's going on?" was all he managed to croak as the ground slipped away. Bewildered, he hung behind her like a towel on a clothesline.

She cocked her head to see how he was doing. "Pull your legs back like the heron. You're dragging." But that only made him begin to wildly flap his arms. "Just relax and soar." Hoping nobody could see them, she moved out over the water and headed upriver, gaining speed and altitude. Finally Ned relaxed and stopped flopping around, and they sailed higher. It was easier than Martha had expected.

"This is incredible," Ned cried as the current lifted them.

Martha was elated. This was like her dream, only better. They soared along the river, Ned holding on and enjoying the view. There was no wind, and their avian perspective, just above the treetops, gave them a glimpse of the world that was anything but ordinary. Seagulls ringed them, riding the currents.

"Scientifically, this isn't possible," Ned called. "I hope you know that."

"Don't think like that," she cautioned, but it was too late. He began to lose altitude, his belief as heavy as the stone in her dream that she'd had to drop. But she couldn't let go of him, and they plummeted down.

"Over there," Martha shouted, pointing to the riverbank and doing her best to stay airborne. "Aim for it." Ned flapped frantically now in an effort to stay up. They tumbled down on soft sand, just missing the water. With Ned pulling, they clambered up the bank. Her slacks got caught in the brambles and tore as she pulled free. On the walkway, they began laughing from sheer exhilaration.

"That was close," Ned sputtered as Martha brushed stickers and bits of foliage off her slacks. "I won't ask how we did that." He dusted off his knees.

"Good, because I don't know. It's a mystery."

"You don't know either?" That made him laugh even harder. They were laughing when Carol and Joe appeared.

"We just saw a couple of huge birds," Carol said. "Couldn't tell what they were." Then she frowned. "How'd you get covered with dirt like that, Ned?" Her words triggered even more hilarity, and now Ned simply gave in to it. He couldn't stop. The experience of flight had filled him with joy and awe, and something in him held locked for a long time released in spontaneous, contagious laughter. Martha gave in to it, too. "What?" Carol sputtered, trying to fight it. Joe smiled, then guffawed. A moment later, they were all laughing hard, until their sides ached and tears streamed down their faces, not knowing what it was about.

Clark stopped by in the morning with the children. They were on their way to the beach with their plastic pails and shovels. He handed his mother a printout. "Here's what I found about the dance. Not much." Martha looked at the page, which said that the jaguar symbolized supernatural forces. Clark had highlighted three things. First, that there were probably some ceremonies and beliefs that were being kept secret, which should be investigated before all traces of them were gone. Much of mask history was a question mark; the traditions existed in remote areas and were not openly shared. Many traditions had simply disappeared. Second, the jaguar (generally called *tigre* in Spanish) undoubtedly was the single most important animal to the indigenous populations of Central and Southern Mexico, and it remained one of the most popular modern mask types. "Its popularity may seem surprising," she read, "when you realize it is almost extinct in Mexico today."

But it was the third item that really struck her: The basic function of masks and masked dances was the transformation of a threatening world into a beneficial one. The masks were used to create profound mystical transformation: the wearer became someone or something else. They arose not only from the relationship humans had with the natural world, but from the deeper relationship with the creative forces of the universe. Since we did not know how the ancient cultures had understood the cosmos, we did not know for certain the symbolism and purpose of the masks. Because the masks were created to connect with the spirit world, they were seen as imbued with magic.

"So your mask may be valuable," Clark said when she finished reading. "It certainly makes you wonder about its history—where it's been, how it was used." But he admitted he had been unable to find out anything about the dance itself. And because he was convinced she was taking Spanish, he suggested the subject might make a good research project for her class. "Maybe you'll have to go to Mexico," he added, rounding up the kids.

As soon as Clark left, Ned came over. He hemmed and hawed for a few minutes as if he didn't want to ask his real question, so she invited him in. "I know you want to ask about flying," she said. "Do you want some tea?" She brewed a pot of Celestial Citrus, thinking that would help him with clarity as much as it had helped her.

"I don't even know what to say," he said as she got out two cups. "How long have you been doing that?"

"Believe it or not, just twenty-four hours."

"You know, when I saw you yesterday I felt there was something special about you. I couldn't put my finger on it, but you seemed to have a sense of confidence and enthusiasm."

"I had just learned how to fly at that moment," she explained, as if it was not at all unusual.

"You must know something about how it happened."

"I know a little bit, but none of it is scientific," she replied. She wanted to trust him, and she wanted to take someone into her confidence. She scarcely knew him but something told her it was OK to share what had happened.

He studied her. "I've lived my whole life by the laws of science," he said, "but to tell you the truth, it hasn't been much fun. The last straw was losing my wife. I thought modern medicine could save her, and it didn't. It's made me question a lot of things."

She returned his gaze, and they sat quietly for a moment with their tea.

"You feel like someone I can trust," he said. "I don't have that feeling with many people, but there's something different about you. Maybe there's a reason I came to visit my sister now. And maybe it has nothing to do with her. I'm going to tell you something I haven't told anyone else. I had almost given up living."

Martha focused on her tea.

"I'm not saying that to depress you," he said. "Or because I want you to fix anything. I'm saying it because after last night I'm ready to put that behind me. I want to hear how you learned to fly."

Chaco growled as she finished telling the story, and Martha looked out the window to see Henry Hocket coming up the walk. She invited him in and introduced him to Ned. "I put together some information for you about the feather," Henry told her, handing her the packet. "This will give you a sense of its value." He nervously shifted his weight, looking briefly at Ned. "I know we didn't get a chance to talk, but if I can answer any questions for you, please let me know."

Once again, Martha noticed she felt uneasy in his presence.

"I was hoping we could set up a time to meet," he continued. "One of my interests in studying the quetzal is to help protect and preserve its habitat, so any information I can get is valuable."

Martha escorted him to the door and thanked him for the information. "I'll give you a call," she said. "Things have been very hectic lately so I haven't had time."

"It's just that—" he stopped, then looked at her as if this was his last-ditch effort. "It would be an incredible opportunity for me scientifically if I had one of the feathers."

"He makes me nervous," she told Ned after Hocket was gone.

"He certainly seems passionate about his research. What's this feather he's interested in?"

"The quetzal gave it to me when he showed me the path," she said, surprised at how open she was being. "No one is supposed to know I have it, but my grandson borrowed it without asking. Now it seems everyone is finding out about it. I was told to keep it safe, and I've blown even that simple request. So far I am not being very responsible with the gifts." She traced a finger around the rim of her mug. "I have always been a responsible person. I never lose my keys or neglect to return a book I've borrowed. But this is a new level of responsibility and I guess I need to learn how to do it. I have so many unanswered questions, I think I need to go to the school."

At the thought of the school she began to worry. "I promised my grandchildren I'd help them start a garden. I'm having trouble fitting all this in."

"Tell you what," Ned said. "I'll till the ground for the garden in exchange for a flying lesson. In fact, I'll weed and prune and water and do whatever else needs to be done. It'll give me something to do and free you up a bit."

Martha smiled and carried the mugs to the kitchen. "Mr. Pine," she said, "prepare for takeoff."

6

Just when she thought she knew something, Martha discovered that she didn't know it after all. She assumed a flying lesson would be as straightforward as preparing a garden plot, but in fact it wasn't. She assumed she could teach someone else to fly, when she barely knew how herself.

¡Ay caramba! Que loco, Chaco muttered, needing to put a stop to this. He leapt onto the counter and—right in front of her—knocked a glass off. It fell to the floor and shattered. She saw it too late to catch it. "What in the name of craziness are you doing?" she said, going to get a broom.

Exactamente, he snorted, but the raspy sound went unnoticed. He waited to see if his diversion had worked. As a master of manifestation, Chaco understood how to make things happen. He knew how to use intention. He could have knocked the glass off the counter without going near it. It was the way of the universe: manifestation followed a clear intention. But Martha would have missed the connection. This way, she might see it. He waited.

He knew that humans usually gummed up the works with personal issues, wishful thinking, and dysfunctional beliefs that made it nearly impossible for them to see clearly. When humans manifested something, they generally attributed it to persistence or luck rather than personal power. "I worked hard on that," they'd say. His personal favorite was "Don't know how I pulled that off."

Humans were schooled in the laws of science and predictability, so it was easy to surprise them. What was challenging was getting their attention. They focused on the past, which was already gone, and thus believed that history repeats itself. They failed to see their powerful and intimate connection with the process of creation. Chaco stared at Martha, thinking he might be here forever until she woke up. He wished he could work with the young one instead. She was a quick study.

"He's trying to tell me something," she told Ned. "My granddaughter said he talks, but for the life of me I can't hear him."

"Maybe you're supposed to put your breakables away before the lesson," Ned suggested.

"I think it's more than that. That's another reason I need to go to the school. By the way, thank you so much for your hard work this morning."

Ned had tilled the ground for the garden, and Melissa and Matthew had planted lettuce and carrots and beans. Afterwards, Martha made a pitcher of lemonade. They sat on a bench to admire their handiwork as Melissa read the signs at the end of each row. Since Chaco's arrival, she had learned to read, amazing her parents. She told her grandmother that Chaco helped her by telling her the words. Martha wanted more details, although remembering Bob the Bear she chalked it up to make-believe and the active imagination of a young child. But then Melissa had turned toward her with the look of a child who is about to ask an important question. "Do you want to know what Chaco's favorite word is?"

"I didn't realize he had one. Of course, yes, please tell me."

"¡Caramba!" she had said with a great deal of flourish for someone so young.

Martha had repeated it slowly as if she couldn't quite believe it. "Caramba. How interesting." She glanced at Chaco, who appeared to be snoozing. "How does he use it?"

"It's Spanish."

"He speaks Spanish?" Martha had asked, not quite believing she was having this conversation.

Melissa then burst into giggles. "Of course he does. How else would he know it?" She said this as if it were obvious and Martha was only three years old.

Martha had let out a sigh. Did she dare go on? "What does he sound like when he talks, dear?"

"Like a cat, grandma, what else?" And then she scampered off. The subject was closed. She gave Chaco a pat on the head and went to draw with her crayons. Chaco opened his eyes and looked at Martha with detachment.

Matthew had learned something new, too—how to juggle. In the gardening store, he found a set of juggling fruit stitched from bright fabric and stuffed with flaxseed. He studied the diagrams in the small booklet after planting the garden and moments later was tossing stuffed oranges wildly into the air.

¡Ay-yay-yay! Chaco had to take cover under a chair to avoid being hit. *Use your intention.* But Matthew didn't hear him either. Humans lost their ability to hear animals and other beings at a young age. Matthew was already trying to convince Melissa that cats don't talk, although Chaco noticed the way that Matthew sometimes studied him. He hadn't completely lost his ability. *Listen to what you know inside. The ability is within.* One of the oranges hit the lampshade. *¡Caramba!* Chaco dashed for the den.

"Have you heard from her?" Olivia asked, stirring a tall glass of iced Celestial Citrus tea.

"I have not," Aurora said. They were having lunch—gazpacho and *bollos*—on the veranda overlooking the garden at the school. "But Chaco believes she will be showing up at any minute. I think this is his biggest challenge to date. It is testing his normally unflappable patience. This will move him into being a master teacher." A hummingbird flitted in the bougainvillea. "I reminded him there is often pain before progress. We don't grow from our comfort, we grow from our discomfort. It is what doesn't work that drives us forward. We discover freedom as we shed our old patterns and leave the past behind. That is exactly where Chaco is positioned. He even asked if he could teach the granddaughter instead because she has not yet forgotten. For her, the world is still magical. Every day it's a mystery, because she doesn't yet have an idea of how it is supposed to be."

"Does it concern you that this is our oldest student yet?"

"Not in the slightest. Age in fact has brought her openness because she has begun to review what hasn't worked. She is not fully aware of her openness, but she can still take advantage of it."

"She relaxed enough to be able to fly," Olivia said, "although for a bit I wondered if I would be able to get her airborne. The existing belief system can make it a challenge, and her beliefs are twentieth century. From the time she was small she was taught to give all of her power away, to believe that she was not wise enough to manage it for herself. It is difficult to overcome that cultural conditioning."

"Difficult but not impossible. We are fortunate to have learned the ancient teachings so that we can pass them on."

"She asked me if I knew why this was happening to her."

"And?" Aurora asked. Both women spoke comfortably and openly, without judgment.

"And I told her that some questions are bigger than any of us can answer. You can see which direction the wind is blowing without knowing where it will go. Sometimes all we know is the direction. The direction takes us where we need to go."

"She's stuck. She hasn't taken action. She's treading water."

"Many of us have done that," Olivia said. "In a pool this deep, however, eventually you have to swim."

"She's teaching the neighbor to fly."

"She sees her power. She knows it's there. She has learned to transfer it to others. The flying lesson will be useful for that reason. In teaching him, she must embrace the power for herself."

"And if she doesn't?" Aurora asked.

"The teaching is also about trust," Olivia replied. "At some point we all have to accept that we don't know. We have to surrender. In the end, it's not about anything that we do. We're facilitators. We simply pass the teachings on. The lost arts are alive. They interact with each of us to awaken us to our full potential."

Aurora studied her for a moment. "You've become an excellent master teacher," she said. "I'm looking forward to working with you with our next batch of students. Steven is too. He'll be teaching Portals this time, by the way. He has a knack for using them, and unlimited energy for chasing those who go off course. And I'm happy you'll be teaching Sensory Arts again. It is one of your gifts."

Olivia decided to pose the question that had been on her mind. "Will you be teaching the Dance of the Jaguar?"

"I don't know yet." Aurora grew pensive. "I don't know if I'll have anyone ready."

"I'd like to assist if you do. I've never seen it."

"Few have seen it," Aurora reminded her. "The dance is never watched. And there is only one human participant. But yes, when the time comes, you can assist in setting up. I will need help preparing the fire."

Martha prepared Ned for his flying lesson in the living room. Chaco came in and surveyed the room for something he could break to create a distraction.

"You have to believe this is possible," Martha said, instructing Ned to stand in the middle of the room. "All you'll do is go up and then come back down. Let's keep it simple." She wished Olivia were there to help because she really didn't know what she was doing.

"Does this chair have a seatbelt?" he asked.

Martha wondered if perhaps she should call the lesson off, but she thought about all the work he had done in the garden. She could offer to cook him dinner instead. "Are you sure you want to try this on your own?"

"Absolutely. This will give me a new lease on life."

"You know, there are responsibilities that come with the gift," she said. "You just can't go flying everywhere without giving something back."

"What are you talking about?"

That was when Martha realized she didn't know what she was talking about. At that moment, however, they heard glass breaking in the den, and they both hurried to see what had happened.

Chaco was sitting in the chair. The window across from him was broken, and a vine dangled inside the room.

Ned let himself out through the sliding glass door. Nothing outside was amiss, but a large vine had grown up by the window, preventing him from getting near it to check. "I don't remember this being here," he said. To Martha, it looked like the vines she had seen in the rainforest, but she didn't realize the small piece Clark had plucked off her sleeve had taken root. When she went back into the den to look around, something on the floor caught her eye, and she bent to pick it up. It was a beautiful carved stone bird, about the size of a fist; she cradled it in her hand.

"What is it?" Ned asked, coming into the den. But she couldn't speak. She just stood there holding the bird, which was familiar to her. She could tell by how it felt in her hand—smooth, heavy, round—that it was the stone she had dropped in her dream.

In one instant its existence blurred the boundaries between this realm and all the others. "This makes everything true," she said, the words tumbling out, "The portal, the flying, the hut in the rainforest, everything. I lost this bird in a dream. I didn't realize it was real. But now here I am, wide awake, finding it." She held the bird against her heart, knowing that once she did, there was no going back. Chaco watched her with renewed interest. When she finally placed the bird on a shelf, she noticed there was a hole in its back for a feather. Her quetzal feather fit perfectly, arcing out majestically.

There was a surge of energy as she placed the feather in position. It was similar to what had happened when she first put the amulet on, but stronger. Like it or not, she was part of something she didn't understand. There were forces interacting with her and she felt drawn, on a deep level, into their cosmic dance. Even though she was afraid, it was time to act. It was time to accept the invitation she had been given and to find out why she was being called. Ned offered to repair her window and left to get the glass.

Liz came by as soon as he left. "I've scarcely heard from you lately," she said. "I was hoping we could go out to a movie one of these nights. What are you up to?"

They walked out to the garden to look at all the flowers and bushes that were coming into bloom. Martha showed her the grandchildren's garden. "What's the vine?" Liz asked. "What happened to your window?"

"It's kind of a long story," Martha said, as Ned reappeared with a pane of glass. Martha made the introductions and when the two women went back into the house Liz said, "Well, there certainly are all kinds of new things going on in your life. No wonder I haven't heard from you."

"It's not what you think," Martha told her.

"He's attractive, he's available, he's the right age, and he's over here doing all kinds of favors for you. It certainly can be what I think," Liz replied.

Martha tried to change the subject but Liz wouldn't let her. "At least tell me you're interested," Liz prompted.

"I don't think he's here for very long. Do you want some tea or something?" She wished she could tell Liz what was going on, but a little voice inside her issued a caution. Chaco, stretched out in a nearby chair, eyed her. *It won't make sense to her. It's outside her realm of comprehension. ¿Comprende?*

"How long has it been since you've been on a date?"

"A while," Martha said. "But you know that."

"So if he asks you out, accept. It'll be fun for you. And heaven knows you need a little fun. Some excitement, too. Maybe that's what that fortune teller meant."

Liz's assumptions had never bothered Martha before. But lately she was noticing lots of new things. It was like waking up to discover she was living in a world she had never really examined. Or questioned.

Ned called out that he was done if she wanted to check his handiwork. "I'm going to get out of the way," Liz said. "But call me later." She winked and headed for the front door.

Ned was already cutting the vine back when Martha went outside. "You don't have to do all that," she said, but he insisted.

"It gives me something to do," he said. "I like to be active. And it gets me out of the house." He gestured toward Carol and Joe's. "Carol means well, being concerned about me and all. But to tell you the truth, I wish she'd stop." He cleared the vine away from the house. "I was thinking," he said, very casually, as if it were nothing at all, "how would you like to take in a movie?"

Despite Liz's hunch, Martha was caught off guard. It was a tempting offer, and a month or two ago, she would have been happy to accept. But now, following the wind, wherever it took her, was on her mind. And it seemed suddenly to be more compelling than anything else. "I would love to go," she said. "In a few days. If you're still here," she added. "And I hope you are. But right now I have to find out what my opportunity is. It seems the planets have aligned and the pull for some reason is irresistible."

It was a new Martha talking. She could feel it, and it enlivened her. He sensed it, too, and even though he'd just met her, he felt the spell of her enthusiasm. "I will be here for a few days," he said. "I can't leave without finding out what happens, that's for sure. And I can't leave without my lesson. I'm not going to forget that you promised to teach my how to fly." He laughed. "You are a very unusual woman. Have you always been like this?"

She laughed too. "No. But I've been like this long enough to discover that I want to know more."

Chaco, watching from the shade of the peony, rolled over and stretched. ¡Caramba! Standing, he shook himself off. For the time being, his work was done. With an *hasta luego* in their direction, he sauntered off.

"Did you hear that?" Martha asked Ned.

"Hear what?"

The yard was empty but Martha knew she had heard someone talking. Reaching up to touch the amulet around her neck, she thought about what Aurora had told her in the hut. Risky or not, whatever this was all about, she could no longer ignore it. She went to get the card from her desk. The time finally had come.

7

The Ancient Wisdom School was located on a narrow street not far from the central plaza in Cuernavaca. The town, known for having one of the most perfect climates in the world—a predictable temperature of 72 degrees nearly every day—had long been called the City of Eternal Spring, and it was once famous for its abundant gardens. Shimmering pink blossoms cascading down a wall caught Martha's eye as she entered the school through an arched door. Behind her the noise of the street faded and tranquility took over, permeating her being. The courtyard was planted with fragrant flowering trees and she inhaled the sweet aroma as she studied her surroundings. Several hundred years earlier, the modest palace had been home to a bishop. Now, behind the walls that sheltered it from the traffic outside, students came to learn the lost arts.

Martha had used her portal with great success, emerging in a museum built over a buried pyramid only a short distance from her destination. In fact, there were no problems except for the museum guard who spotted her with an overnight bag and motioned that bags were prohibited in the building. She thanked him for showing her directly to the exit, and she was glad the cab driver had taken American money.

She spied someone sitting on a bench under a tree, reading, and headed that way.

"Can you tell me where I might find—"

"Aurora?" The young man pointed to the left, where the walk led to another courtyard and beyond that, to a garden with a swimming pool. Martha had her choice of two doors, and she debated momentarily about which one to choose. The first one led into a spacious room that seemed to be an office. There were windows overlooking the garden and the pool, and several beautiful leather chairs. She was gazing out the window when she heard a familiar voice.

"You're here! No trouble finding us?" Aurora breezed into the room, greeting her warmly, and Martha felt as glad to see her this time as she had been the first time in the rainforest. Aurora, too, was happy.

"It was much easier this time," Martha admitted. "I knew where I was going." She gestured at her surroundings. "This is absolutely beautiful and so peaceful. I feel like I want to stay forever. I can't believe I was so reluctant to come." Once again, she found herself being very open with Aurora.

"It has that effect on people. We've been in this location for ten years," Aurora explained. "It's somewhat more central than our last school, which necessitated a burro ride through the mountains."

Martha felt grateful to miss that experience, but it made her wonder anew if she was cut out for this. She had not forgotten that Aurora had said *risky*.

Aurora smiled in a reassuring way. "This gives us more access to students, and we find them to be just as dedicated," she continued, setting some papers down. "We'll begin as soon as you're ready. If you go through the other door, you'll find your room, where you can leave your things. Then you can join us for the class."

Following the instructions, Martha found herself in a narrow arched hallway lit with sconces. The third door bore her name printed on a card. Her room was small but inviting. The window looked out on the aquamarine pool and the garden with its rainbow of flowering vines. There were fresh flowers on the antique table and the bed was neatly made. She hung her sweater on the back of the chair, washed her hands with the fragrant soap in the bathroom, and went to begin her first class, Introduction to the Ancient Arts.

There were about twenty students in the room, and she found a seat in the second row. She had to step over a backpack, and a gangly young man shrugged an apology. He had a notebook, and the name on the front said Roger Ray. The lecture was just beginning, and as she looked in her purse for a pen and something to write on, Aurora explained that it was an oral tradition, so there were no books. "You won't need to take notes, either," she said, smiling at Martha. "Everything is absorbed and becomes a part of who you are."

That sounded simple enough, and Martha hoped her memory would cooperate. Roger opened his notebook and began to scribble notes anyway, evidently not believing what Aurora had said.

"All of you have chosen to be here," Aurora continued. "Because of that we welcome you to this opportunity to relearn skills that were once, ages ago, a part of our lives." Introductions were made, and Martha was surprised to learn that most of the students had taken conventional transportation, not having yet learned to use portals. Most were quite a bit younger. When Aurora described Martha's experience in the rainforest, several of them gasped. Using portals was evidently one of the more challenging classes, and one that occasionally led to students getting lost for a day or two before someone could find them.

"You obviously have the gift," the young woman next to Martha said. Her name was Angela. "You'll have to be my partner. I'm terrified of getting lost. A friend of mine took the class and ended up in Poland when everybody else went to Egypt. She had to take a plane home."

"I'm new to all this," Martha replied, still not having much of a clue how she did it. "I'm happy to be your partner, but I make no guarantees. Bring a sandwich and your passport, just in case. If you knew how topsy-turvy my life was lately, you might be wise to pick someone else, for your own safety."

"We won't be starting with portals," Aurora continued. "So you can all relax. After the introduction we'll move right into Basic Arts. Eventually you'll be creating everything you need, from money to love, but initially we'll work on easy things, like chocolate. Chocolate is very easy to create."

"Yum," said Angela, who looked as if she did not have to watch her weight. "I'll be happy if that's all I learn."

"I call it creating but it's actually manifestation," Aurora said. "But I'm getting ahead of myself. First, the introduction." The rest of the morning passed quickly, with Aurora's melodic voice describing the work of the school to teach the lost arts.

They broke briefly for lunch in the garden by the pool, where they were served zucchini flowers and rice, an assortment of fruits and something called *dulce de mansana*, which Martha thoroughly enjoyed. She was surprised to see Chaco pass through the garden as she was talking with Angela. He glanced at her but kept going as if he had things to do. "I've been taking correspondence courses," Angela was saying. "I decided it was finally time to do the hands-on."

During the Basic Arts class in the afternoon, they were introduced to beginning manifestation. Martha thought she understood the concept, but she had no idea how to actually do it. Aurora explained that as they started to practice, it would become clearer. "Most of what you will be learning is difficult for the mind to grasp. That's why it is important to recognize that the mind is only one tool." She went on to explain that the body has multifaceted sensory capabilities. "Open yourselves to receiving and sending energy in new ways rather than relying on conventional techniques. Observe what happens. Especially be aware of your heart and what it is telling you. Begin to listen with your heart. Begin to act from your heart."

To learn to manifest, she said, they would begin with the idea of creativity. "Creativity is innate, as much a part of us as breathing. It arises naturally and is called a desire for self-expression. We are expressing not only something within us, but also something bigger that we are a part of." Roger turned to a new page in his notebook, momentarily distracting Martha. Another student shifted in his chair.

But Aurora's energy had a calming effect, quieting everyone and moving them deeper into the still pool of awareness. "Your culture," she said, "values science over art or spirit. It values product over process. It values commercial over natural. You have accepted those beliefs but have you considered how you feel about them?" She moved around the room as she talked, watching the reactions as she spoke. "The act of creating satisfies two desires: the personal desire for permanence as well as the community desire for inspiration. It's an exchange," she said. "You share your vision of the world and are inspired by the vision of others. That is the way we all grow." Then she explained that there was another reason to create. "You may have heard about the tradition of dances in this part of the world. They were not performed for the public." Her eyes took in the room. "They were done to recognize and interact with the spirit world—some call this the metaphysical world. The ancients did not view science as separate from art, and the world of spirit was ever present in their daily life. The natural world was their television, the magic screen where figures of light took shape and spoke."

Roger had stopped taking notes. Aurora pulled several animal masks from the cabinet at the back of the room and hung them on the wall. "Everything existed in relationship to something else," she said. "The dances were used to establish balance and harmony with all of creation. We are not going to focus on masks, but I want you to be aware of this background. I want you to be aware of the fact that what we call creativity or art grew out of the relationship humans had with everything around them, both seen and unseen. These were functional pieces imbued with power that represented the mystery of the unknown." Then she told them they would be creating something to represent their vision.

"What if we don't know what our vision is?" a young woman named Sheila asked.

"Trust that you do know," Aurora answered. "Do you feel something inside, some stirring, something pushing you to discover your personal truth?" When Sheila nodded, Aurora continued. "That feeling is the knowledge inside you waking up. That is why you're here, to learn to stop resisting what you know. We've learned to resist our own truth." A frown formed on Sheila's face, and Martha wondered when she could ask about the connection between dreams and reality.

"Just keep listening. Trust yourself. You don't have to figure it out. At some moment it will just click." Aurora scanned the room. "How many of you feel that no one knows the real you?" Several hands shot up. "Why do you think that is?" Her tone was neither threatening nor judgmental.

"Because we don't share who we really are," a young man in the back said.

Aurora nodded in encouragement. "And why not?"

"It's not safe," he continued. "We might get laughed at, or it might get used against us somehow." Martha watched Roger jot notes again and thought about not being able to tell Liz where she was. The experience was fresh in her mind and made her uncomfortable. She didn't feel any need to make notes about it.

"Most people feel it is not safe to speak the truth. So they close that up inside," Aurora said. "Where it seems protected. But then what is the result?"

"We feel alone," Angela said.

"Yes. And we begin to believe we are alone. Then we suffer because of that belief. But I want you to look at a bigger picture. Look at our interconnection. It is essential. It's what drives the process." Roger began to scribble even faster.

Angela turned to Martha and smiled as Aurora's words sank in. "It makes sense, don't you think?"

Martha's mind was beginning to go blank.

"You're here to connect with your power," Aurora continued. "In the process of growing up you've been disconnected from it. At first it will feel unfamiliar and intimidating, as if you've hitched a ride on a tornado." She made a spinning motion with her finger.

Angela leaned forward and instinctively put her hands over her face. Roger looked pale. Mulling over this new information, Martha decided it made the burro ride sound like a piece of cake.

"In the beginning you don't know where it's going to take you or what it's capable of," Aurora went on. "But your power is a part of you, an innate part, and as you embrace it and learn to use it, it will come to feel natural. Eventually, using it will be as natural as breathing."

"How long does that take?" Sheila asked.

"That depends entirely on you. You can jump right in or you can test the water with your toes until you get used to it. We'll go into this in more detail later."

Roger shifted in his chair. "Is there a possibility for serious injury?"

"We always advise caution," Aurora said, "especially if you feel any doubt. You will never be asked to do anything you are not able to do," she said carefully. "But trusting yourself is essential. It's also essential to trust that you are capable of doing far more than you have ever considered. We are here to show you the possibilities." She looked around the room. "For now, step one. Let's manifest chocolate!"

For the remainder of the afternoon, they practiced. Martha, after several false starts, manifested truffles, much to her delight. Sheila manifested a plate of divinity, which—even though it wasn't chocolate—just happened to be her favorite. Angela manifested chocolate-covered almonds. The only failure was Roger's. Aurora said he was trying too hard, and it wasn't a matter of trying. Everyone knew that if you couldn't manifest chocolate, you couldn't continue, and Roger was unable to manifest Milky Ways. "It's not up to me," Aurora said. "Relax and trust. That's all you can do." Roger was downcast.

Sheila tried to console him over dinner.

"How did you do it?" He appeared close to desperation.

"I really can't say. I just followed the directions."

"I followed them, too, but nothing happened." He grew more morose with every passing minute. "Drat. I thought for sure I'd be able to do the easy things. Now I'll never get to Portals."

"I don't think any of it is easy," said Martha, who was eavesdropping. "And I don't have a clue how I do it. It just happens."

¡Ay-yay-yay! Sooner or later you must own your power.

She had an odd sensation of being watched and she turned to see Chaco. She still wished she could talk to him like Melissa did.

It doesn't just happen.

"You know, maybe it doesn't just happen," she told Roger. "I make it happen by connecting with my power. I am not entirely sure how, but I am definitely doing it." Inside, she noticed an expanded sense of confidence she had never felt before.

Exactamente. Time for a siesta.

After dinner Sheila, Roger and Angela went for a walk outside. Martha and Steven, who taught the Power Arts, followed along behind. It was a shock emerging into the city. The energy felt chaotic and unfocused. Drivers honked impatiently. "Why don't they just decide they will drive home with no problems?" Martha asked. "I bet they all anticipated traffic, so there it is. They created it." She felt energized by the evening air. The sun was going down over the hills and they stopped to watch as the city moved around them.

"There's something magical about the sunset," Angela said as the air turned lavender.

"It's a time of transition," Steven noted. "It's a natural ritual that marks the end of the day, the end of the light. We are moving into darkness and dreamtime. The melding is what's magical, the brief moment between light and dark when there is no separation between the two worlds."

"Interesting," Angela said. "I never thought about all that. It makes sense."

"It makes sense because you know it inside already. My role as a teacher is simply to bring your knowledge into your awareness, to put you in touch with it again. That's what the Power Arts are about."

"I want a Milky Way," Roger said. No sooner did he say it than he saw one lying in the street. It had been run over and the wrapper was torn, but it was a Milky Way nonetheless. Roger was jubilant. He picked up the flattened candy bar and held it against his chest. "I did it, I manifested."

"I'll vouch for it," Steven said. "But keep practicing. You've got the idea, but your technique needs some work."

8

Thinking she heard a sound when she woke up, Martha held her breath to listen. The darkness played tricks with her eyes as she stared into it, trying to see. It took her a moment to realize where she was. Her heart was pounding in her ears, but the room was deathly silent.

The vivid and disturbing images of her dream seemed real: she was in the rainforest. Someone was chasing her. The forest seemed impassable. Out of the shadows arose dozens of disembodied animal masks. She needed her quetzal plume but she couldn't find it. Terrified, she called out for help. Finally she pulled herself awake and realized she was safe. Or was she?

Something bumped her bed. She reached for her lamp so fast that her trembling hands toppled it, and when the light came on she saw Chaco at the foot of her bed.

Evidently he had come in through the open window. Relieved, she took a deep breath and tried to calm down. She fluffed her pillow, wondering if she would be able to go back to sleep. But Chaco looked at her so intently that it put her on edge. "What is it?" she asked, still trying to shake off the dream.

¡Ay! You called.

She leaned over so she could see the clock on the nightstand; the luminous dial read midnight. She had only been asleep for an hour. "I wish I knew what was going on."

You were searching for the solution in dreamtime so you will have it when you need it. He looked back over his shoulder as if something had caught his attention. *It is one way to do it. You are dreaming your power.*

She yawned with sleepiness. "I wish I could understand you."

Esta bien. Go back to sleep. You will find the solution. You are very close to it. He disappeared the way he had come.

But she couldn't go back to sleep. Something bothered her but she couldn't put her finger on it. For some reason she wanted the quetzal feather, which she'd left at home. She climbed out of bed and got a drink of water. She was groggy, but she knew she wouldn't sleep until she went on her mission. It wouldn't take long. As she got dressed, there was a knock at her door followed by a woman's voice. She hurried to answer. "I hope I didn't scare you," Angela whispered, coming in. "I couldn't sleep. I saw your light."

"I had an odd dream that woke me up." Martha rubbed her eyes, stifling another yawn. "I'm just going to run home for a minute."

"It's the middle of the night!" Angela exclaimed. "Can't it wait till morning?" Martha held a finger to her lips to remind her that others might be sleeping. Angela's next suggestion, that she consult Aurora, fell on deaf ears.

"I don't want to disturb anyone," Martha explained. "It only takes a second to pop home through the portal. I'll be back before anyone misses me. If I can just get to the museum…"

"There's a portal here," Angela said. "I overheard Steven telling Sheila about it."

Martha ran a comb through her hair. "Do you know where?"

"In the courtyard. It's the one they use for the class. Roger and I were checking it out earlier."

"Show me." She slipped on her shoes, relieved that she didn't have to make her way through the city. "You're a lifesaver. I'm glad you stopped by."

"This is what we talked about in class," Angela said, excited. "You're already creating what you need. I decided to go for a walk because I couldn't sleep, and I noticed your light. Before this class I wouldn't have made that connection. I would have just told you it was lucky I stopped by." She paused, quickly plotting something. "I'll show you on one condition. Take me with you."

"What?" Martha grappled with what to say. She felt reluctant to agree, but at the same time she wanted to know where the portal was. "I've never used a portal with anyone else," she cautioned. "I have no idea how it's done."

"We'll give it a shot. If it doesn't work, you can go alone. I want to see what it's like. It's the one thing I want to learn more than anything else. Besides, won't you feel better not being alone?"

Martha admitted she would.

"Then it's settled. Let's go."

"Don't you want shoes? Or clothes?"

Angela shook her head. She had pulled a sweatshirt on over her cotton pajamas and slipped on a pair of flip-flops for her walk. "We're just going to your house. And it's dark. Who will see us?"

Martha grabbed her cell phone, and then, like a teenager, put a pillow in her bed and pulled the blanket up over it, something she'd never done in her life. Moments later they were in the deserted courtyard, two shadows stealing through the night.

"Here," Angela whispered. Martha stood by a stone she had noticed earlier.

"Hold on. And think about my house," Martha told her. There was a rush of air and Martha knew they'd done it. She hoped it wasn't a mistake to take Angela with her.

"Oh my gosh!" Angela was jumping up and down. "It worked! Look. But you didn't tell me you lived on a farm."

"I don't." Martha warily surveyed their surroundings. They were in the middle of a field. Not far away, a herd of cows was heading their way, tails swinging. The sun was just coming up.

Watching their step, they traipsed through wet grass toward a small, tidy farmhouse and some outbuildings. A farmer was coming out of the barn. "Good morning," Martha called. Angela hung back, wishing she had taken Martha's advice about getting dressed.

"What have we here?" He cocked his head. "You're a long way from home. Slept in the car evidently." His dog bounded over, tail wagging, and Angela bent to pet it.

"Can you tell us where we are?" Martha asked.

"Cornwall. Where do you think?" He continued with his chores.

"England?" Her surprise made him take a step back.

He scanned the field behind them for clues. "There's no roads back there at all," he finally said. "How did you get here?"

As Martha considered what to say, Angela spoke. "We used a portal."

"Did you now? That's a good one. I can't wait to tell the missus." He chuckled. But he also tried to peer around Martha for a better look at Angela. Martha introduced herself but suddenly realized she didn't know Angela's last name.

"Leigh. Angela Leigh," Angela said, poking her head around Martha.

The farmer studied them with curiosity and finally held out a weathered hand. "William Bole." He led them in the direction of the house where his wife, not expecting company, was cleaning up the kitchen. There was bread rising in a large crockery bowl on the stove, and the yeasty aroma filled the room. "Mary, we've visitors. Came through a portal, they did." He winked at his wife.

"A what? Sorry for the mess, I wasn't expecting anyone. Sit down. Would you like some tea? A biscuit?" She studied Angela's pink pajamas. "Oh, a pretty fabric."

Angela cheerily thanked her, as if intercontinental travel in a pair of pajamas was not the least bit unusual. Martha checked her watch. It was a few minutes past midnight. "We don't want to trouble you. How far is the nearest town?"

"Ten miles." William Bole turned to leave. "I'll be heading in this afternoon if you want a ride."

"I'm not going into any town dressed like this," Angela interjected, turning to Martha to plead her case. "Even if no one knows me. I've never been to England. I finally get here and look at me. I can't even sightsee." Her face clouded over. "This is all my fault. You would have been fine by yourself."

"This isn't a sightseeing trip," Martha reminded her. "We have to get back."

But Angela continued to fret. "What if we'd ended up in London? I would have been absolutely mortified. Just the thought of it is horrifying." She shuddered.

Martha, who was trying to formulate a plan, shushed her.

"American, are you?" Mary, who seemed happy to have visitors, set about making them something to eat.

But Martha, after mulling things over, suddenly had an idea. "Something Aurora said," she explained to Angela. Excited, she told Mary they had to go.

"Stay and have your tea," Mary pleaded, enjoying the diversion they had created. "And a biscuit. I can't send you off hungry. It's not polite." She was drawn to the women, and she wanted to know more about them, especially Martha, who was about her age and glowed like the peach rose in her garden. To Mary, she represented courage.

"We don't have time," Martha said, hurrying out the door. "We have to get back before they miss us." Angela followed, trying to run in her flip-flops.

Mary wrapped two biscuits in a napkin and chased after them. "Take these with you," she called. William came out of the barn to see what was up. Out in the field, Martha instructed Angela to hold onto her arm. Mary handed Angela the biscuits and began to shoo curious cows away. William watched as he worked on mending a fence, keeping an eye out but not wanting to be involved.

"Perhaps we'll meet again," Martha told Mary, "when I'm not in such a rush. My apologies, but this is urgent."

"Next time, I'll have regular clothes," Angela said, smiling. "Something nice. I have some very nice things."

Martha interrupted. "Pay attention. We will never get back if you don't stop yammering."

Mary, who had turned to encourage one of the cows to keep moving, turned back to find the women gone. "Wait! Take me!" she wanted to call, but the words wouldn't come. William came running over to grab her; he held her as tightly as he could. "I can't breathe," she finally said. "If you don't mind." Then, without another word, she went back into the house, having witnessed something she couldn't explain. Deep inside, she felt an opportunity had come and gone. How many of those had there been? Sadness welled up in her, and she began to cry. Never again, she vowed. The next time, she would not let fear stop her.

She saw something on the floor and bent to pick it up. It was a business card. One of the women must have dropped it. She looked at the name printed on it: The Ancient Wisdom School. She walked over to her recipe box on the counter and carefully tucked the card inside, where it would be safe.

Their next stop was a small village outside of Hamburg, Germany, where a small boy playing in his yard stared at them. Then Istanbul, followed by Dunedin, New Zealand. Then Sanibel Island off the Gulf Coast of Florida. "We're making progress," said Martha, who wished she had more time to explore. "I'll have my biscuit, if you don't mind." It was almost five in the morning, and the beach they were on was deserted. The restaurant nearby was closed, but they had read the menus posted outside to discover where they were. Martha, who wished she could order scrambled eggs to go with her biscuit, took her shoes off and waded into the warm gulf water. She had given up on going home, but she hoped to get back to the school before the morning class.

"Do you think we'll make it?" Angela asked, sitting down on the shell-covered beach. She had lost one of her flip-flops somewhere.

"Of course," Martha answered. "Sooner or later."

"We could call for help on your phone. Yikes!" One of the shells she had picked up was alive.

"Not yet. No reason to wake everybody."

"I'm really sleepy."

"You must stay awake if you're traveling with me."

Angela rested her head on her knees and closed her eyes. Martha took in the wide night sky brimming with bright stars. The immensity and magic of it calmed her and made her realize life was bigger than her own small problems. She thought for a moment: here she was zipping around the world, far from the comfort and safety of her home. A month ago, she would never in her wildest dreams have thought this possible. How we limit ourselves by our beliefs, she thought, suddenly envisioning Aurora hundreds of miles away in the school. *You will create what you need. The moment of creation will be effortless, as in a dream.*

"I'm ready," Martha said, rousing Angela, who had fallen asleep. "You'll be back in your bed in a moment. Focus on it." Angela, groggy, stood up next to Martha and took hold. Martha felt like she was getting the hang of this. Each time was easier. She kept her awareness on the school in Mexico.

This time Martha knew exactly where she was—in the museum. At last they were back, almost. The museum was dark, and Martha began to worry they were stuck there until it opened. "We have to find an emergency exit," she told Angela. Down one hall they went, and then another. One door led out onto a balcony, but Martha didn't feel like jumping.

They made their way downstairs to the main entrance, just as a guard appeared. "Halt!" he cried in Spanish, giving chase. Angela translated his shouted words about calling the police as they ran back up the stairs. Suddenly Martha had an idea. She pushed through the door onto the balcony and they ran to the railing and swung their legs over. The guard burst through the door, waving a pistol. With a rush of adrenaline Martha grabbed Angela by the hand.

"Jump," she shouted as the guard fired a shot and Angela screamed.

A moment later they were standing in the courtyard. Martha brushed herself off, immensely relieved. True, she had not gotten home, but she was somewhere familiar and no one was shooting at her. She had no idea, falling through the air after their jump, if her plan would work, but it did. She had been able to fly with Angela over the rooftops. The sky was turning lavender and pink and it was beautiful beyond description. The aroma of garlic and olive oil and tortillas wafted up, making her very hungry. Angela was exhausted and Martha trundled her off to get some sleep.

But Martha went to sit in the garden. It thrilled her to be fully present and in touch with a new part of herself. She was alive in a new sense, as if every cell of her body was being called on to act. Some primeval force had been awakened. She was no longer operating on autopilot, simply going through the motions of living. Joy coursed through her, fueling her desire to know what she was truly capable of. She felt ready—really ready—to push past the limitations she had always accepted.

She was too excited to sleep, so she showered and went to breakfast by the pool. She had envisioned a tempting breakfast, and she found a large table spread with platters of sliced tropical fruits and scrambled eggs and toast. Roger soon joined her, still excited by the Milky Way bar he'd found in the street. Martha had almost forgotten about it. It seemed like ages ago, but it was only last night. She couldn't tell Roger that she'd been on a whirlwind tour of the world since then. It would only depress him. The other students filtered in, making short work of the food. Aurora appeared, announcing they would begin the first class of the morning, Reconnecting Arts, outside. Martha was glad; the warm sun felt good on her skin as it crept up over the buildings.

"Did everyone sleep well?" Aurora asked nonchalantly. There were nods, and Roger said he slept like a log. "Did anyone not sleep?" Martha shifted in her seat, wondering if she had been found out. Angela was nowhere to be seen. "Martha?"

Heads turned expectantly to look and Martha debated about telling her story. Then she realized she didn't have a choice. The point of coming to the school was to learn as much as she could. Besides, Aurora obviously knew. She briefly described her dream, Chaco's visit, and the resultant world tour. Roger thought she was making it up.

¡Ay caramba! Chaco materialized at the mention of his name. *Leave me out of it.*

"He came to dreamtime to assist you," Aurora said, "and to show you how to find a solution. When you woke up, he left the dream as well. We will study this later."

Once again, Martha was lost. How could she find an answer in a dream? She suspected everything would be a lot simpler if she could understand Chaco.

"I can't stress enough," Aurora said as Angela walked in, "that the portals can be unpredictable. When you use them, your intention must be crystal clear. You should not be taking anyone with you at this point. It is extremely difficult for a Level 1 to take someone. You did surprisingly well. Angela, any comments?" Angela, still wearing one flip-flop, shook her head.

"We'll focus on extrasensory perception tomorrow," Aurora said, "especially sending and receiving messages. Until then, if you're in doubt about a message you receive, I encourage you to ask for assistance." Angela shot a glance at Martha. "I must commend you both," Aurora added, "for getting back so quickly. It could have been worse." She looked around the hushed room. "It is not unheard of that we have to send the Trackers out." Roger's face fell into his hands as he realized he had a new worry.

"One last thing," Aurora said. "The local police are looking for you, so I would suggest that for the remainder of your time here, you stay inside the school. Angela, too."

They moved on to discuss Reconnecting Arts. Once again, Aurora's voice drifted out into the room with a soothing, calming effect, and everyone settled into a deep state of absorption. "I talked to you yesterday about learning to know your own call. Your call is learned from your family and passed down from your ancestors. Over time, human calls have become damaged as we've lost our connection to the rhythm and cycle of nature and stopped listening to our inner innate wisdom. We've adapted to artificial circumstances—alarm clocks and telephones and electric lights—and grown dependent on technology. Now, I am not saying there is anything wrong with technology," she said as a man's hand went up, and then back down. "It's very useful in a multitude of ways. But we need to not lose the skills we once had because of technology, because these are the skills that make our lives rich and meaningful."

A discussion broke out about the skills humans have lost and how to get them back. Everyone had ideas about which skills they wanted. Aurora cautioned that not everyone develops all the skills to the same degree or at the same pace. "The hope is that over time, humans begin to regain these techniques."

After a few minutes, Aurora picked up where she had left off. "With practice, you will begin to recognize that calls are distinct. As you listen, you will decide which parts of a person's call you want to respond to. You may decide, for instance, that you don't want to respond to a part that wants to argue or blame or defend a position of being right. You might choose instead to simply acknowledge the part that feels unnoticed or unloved. Reconnection is acknowledging the source of everything as you experience it in yourself and others. When you do this you will feel the source expanding in yourself, and you will see it expanding in others."

They did several practice exercises to learn this technique. Roger worried about getting it wrong. "It's like learning to ride a bike,"

Aurora said. "You are mastering balance. When it clicks, you will feel as if it's the most natural thing in the world."

"Well, it's not clicking very fast," Roger told Martha.

Angela still looked slightly haggard at lunchtime. "You better have some coffee," Roger suggested. "We're doing Portals next."

Angela groaned. "I don't want to see another portal for at least a week."

9

During Portals class, Martha got Steven's permission to zip home for a few minutes while he went over basic techniques with the rest of the group. Chaco was sitting in the garden with her grandchildren when she arrived.

"Goodness, are you here alone?"

"No, grandma," Melissa said, stating the obvious. "Chaco's here."

"Where is your father?" She unlocked her door.

"At work. We have a babysitter."

"And where is she?"

"At home talking on the phone," Matthew said, emphasizing every syllable to show his frustration. "Melissa wanted to see the garden."

"Well, I am glad you arrived safely, but it's not a good idea to come without asking," Martha said. "Does your babysitter know where you are?"

Matthew grinned slyly. "No. Now she'll get in trouble. I don't like her. She never plays with us." He stirred the dirt with a stick.

"Look, grandma," Melissa said, pointing. "I planted marshmallows."

"I see that," her grandmother said, noticing several white tops sticking out of the ground.

"Chaco said you would come." Melissa went over to give the cat a hug. "He's smart."

"She thinks he talks," Matthew said, feeling a sense of superiority over his sister because of his age.

"He does talk," Melissa countered, her face clouding over. "Doesn't he, grandma?"

"Cats don't talk," Matthew stated emphatically, "and everyone knows it."

"Matthew, could you go in and get the milk out? We can have milk and cookies."

"Cats don't talk and bears don't talk," he said over his shoulder, disappearing into the house.

"Did you fly here?" Melissa squinted in the sun as she looked up at her grandmother. "Chaco said."

"Oh my." Martha sat down on the bench to regain her composure. "I'm not sure he should be telling you that, dear."

"He told me you were gone."

"Did he say where I was?"

"On an important trip. He said you can fly."

"I see," Martha said.

"I won't tell. Will you teach me? I want to fly."

"Perhaps when you're older. Where would you go if you could fly?"

"Maybe I would fly to school. Or to the moon. Or to where Chaco lives." Martha asked where he lived, and Melissa said it was a long ways away.

"I think he's talking to you too much," Martha said.

"I like when he talks," Melissa replied. "I know big people don't believe in stuff like that. But I do."

"Yes, I can see that."

"And you do."

"Well, yes, I do. I didn't used to."

"I'm going to be just like you when I grow up, grandma." Melissa ran into the house to get a cookie. "C'mon, before Matthew eats them all."

While the children had a snack, Martha telephoned the sitter to tell her where they were. Then she called Leslie on her cell phone. She had just finished grocery shopping and said she would come at once. She arrived at the same moment Clark did.

"Everything's under control," Martha said.

"Chaco took care of us," Melissa said happily.

"He did a very nice job," Martha agreed.

"Mom. Don't encourage her. Between Bob the bear and this cat, we've got more than our share of talking animals. She should be growing out of that by now."

Martha didn't have a chance to argue, because suddenly Matthew appeared to ask where the feather was. "It's extinct," he said. "That man said so."

"It's not extinct yet," Martha explained, hearing her name called. Seconds later Angela walked in. "I did it! I found your house on the first try. I've mastered portals—oh, you have company," she said.

Surprised, Martha made the introductions. "Angela is a new friend," she said. When Clark asked how they met, she said, "In a class we're taking."

"Spanish?" Clark asked, shaking hands with Angela.

"No," she said. "Lost arts." But Clark was rounding up the children to leave. Angela turned to Martha. "We need to get going. We'll be late."

Moments later, Angela accompanied Martha back to the school, and this time they succeeded in going directly. Steven checked them off the list as Angela and Sheila compared notes about how well they had done. Tension grew in the afternoon as they waited for Roger to return, and when they sat down for dinner, he was still missing. Aurora told them not to worry, that he would eventually turn up. But Martha wondered, given his spate of failures, if they shouldn't be more concerned.

Her cell phone rang early the next morning and she fumbled for it. Clark's voice sounded urgent. "Henry did some research and has just told me it is illegal to possess one of the quetzal feathers. So now I'm concerned. The last thing you need is for some federal agency to show up at your door."

Martha was not quite awake. "Who? What?" He repeated the information and she said, "Perhaps you can call me later with all the details. When I'm up."

But he continued, obviously stirred up. "He said he's obligated to report it...." His voice faded out.

She held the receiver closer to her ear. "What?"

"...hoping to talk to you first."

"You're fading in and out."

She heard silence, signaling they had been disconnected. She sat up in bed, propping her pillow behind her. When the phone rang again she walked over to stand by the window. "Could he come this afternoon?" Clark asked.

"I don't understand the urgency," she said.

"People have seen it and talked about it. I guess that's all it takes for some official to get wind of it. I think you need to be smart."

Martha said she would be home by four. "But you need to come with him," she told Clark, feeling her uneasiness return.

Questions hounded her as she got up and pulled on her clothes. Did she need to be concerned? On her way to breakfast, as she thought about telling Aurora what had happened, she learned that Roger had returned. The others had collected to hear his story, and as she came into the courtyard, she saw him by the portal. His shirt was torn and he was clutching a baseball. "You should have seen it," he said. "I was in the outfield and he hit the ball right to me. I got it on the fourth bounce. I started to run and everyone started chasing me, including the cops. I barely got out of there."

"You were on CNN," Steven said. "It was a Yankees game."

Roger stared at his baseball. "I wish I could have gotten it autographed," he sighed. "Then I'd have proof."

"Where else did you go?" Angela asked, relieved that someone else had a potentially more embarrassing story than hers.

Aurora interrupted. "Class, everyone. You can hear the details later."

Olivia Paz was teaching Sensory Arts, and Martha was looking forward to the discussion of extrasensory perception. She had noticed that sometimes she would hum a song and then turn on the radio to discover it was playing. And occasionally she would receive a phone call from someone when she thought about the person.

In class, she learned it went well beyond that. According to Olivia, we have the ability to communicate not only with other humans, but with animals, and even with beings in other dimensions. Martha wondered if that's why she still talked to Murray. They did some simple exercises to practice. "The more clear you are, the more you will send and receive," Olivia said. "In other words, if your mind is cluttered with worry and meaningless chatter, it will be harder for you to pay attention to the signals you are receiving. They won't have as much impact." Her eyes scanned the room to see if everyone was with her. "In part, also, it's learning to trust the information you do receive," she continued. "Practice is essential. Learn to act on what you hear, and you'll begin to hear more."

"What's the best way to develop this ability?" Roger asked. He had put the baseball in his backpack and was taking notes again.

"You'll develop your ability by using it. All of you, your skills are intact, but they are rusty. Eventually, you will discover the cosmos is communicating with you all the time in very useful ways."

Martha pondered the idea of being intimately connected to a living, breathing, pulsing cosmos that was always communicating with her. Maybe that's why she enjoyed gardening and looking at the stars. Maybe when she thought about watering her plants they were actually sending her a message about needing water.

The afternoon class was even more intriguing. It was called Alignment Arts, and no one knew what it would be about. They were brimming with anticipation over lunch. "I hope I can master it," Roger said, making reference to his troubling candy bar experience.

"You've been able to do everything else," Sheila reminded him.

"I'm always the last one to get it," he said.

"Technique arises at the very moment you are ready for it," said Steven, who'd been eavesdropping. "When you are unsure of yourself, you keep yourself from being ready. As you gain mastery, you will gain confidence, and you will discover that abilities come to you more readily because you don't stop them."

"I guess that makes sense," Roger acknowledged.

"You guess? Or you're sure?" Sheila asked.

"I did it again, didn't I?" Roger said, shaking his head as something clicked inside him. "Oh, I see what you're saying. My doubt is holding me back."

"Yes, your doubt, your belief about what you can do," Steven said. "The reason it's important for you to be at the school is to spend time in a field of greater awareness than your own. You are taking advantage of that right now. It is giving you clarity and helping you see. That exposure allows you to internalize it and make it your own."

They eagerly filed into Alignment Arts after lunch. Steven waited until everyone was seated to begin. "Obviously, all I'm giving you today is an introduction," he said. "This is an advanced technique, and you'll be returning to the school as you master the other techniques to learn more about this. By then you'll be Level 2s." He surveyed the room with penetrating eyes. "The technique is ancient," he said. "And for many years it was lost. But it has recently been discovered again, and it is now available to us in a simpler form, one that doesn't take years to learn."

There was a collective sigh of relief from the class.

"Alignment Arts is about aligning yourself with intention and flow. As you work with the techniques you have been learning, you will become increasingly clear about why you are here and what it is you want to do. Then, working with intention, you will consciously put yourself in the flow."

"What is that?" Sheila asked.

"Flow is the force that sustains us. It is the source of everything."

"If we're already a part of it, why do we have to put ourselves in it?"

"That's a good question, Angela," Steven said. "We're in it already, but most of us bob around like a bottle in the ocean, without much control. We believe we're in control, but actually we're at the mercy of our limiting belief system. As we change our belief system, we experience more fulfilling lives. When we live with awareness and don't limit our potential with negative beliefs, we expand from a limited experience into our dream. We experience connection and happiness." His eyes scanned the room to make sure everyone was with him.

"Now, when you surrender to living your dream, you create a positive working relationship with the universe. Work becomes play. Your life becomes effortless. Your days seem magical in terms of synchronicity because you are creating what you need. You are able to see your thoughts take physical form as you dream the shape of your life. You see that you are living in a dynamic, connected, responsive universe."

He could tell by the hush in the room that the ideas were resonating with everyone, and he paused to give them time to absorb the information. Then he suggested they work on techniques.

"It will take you a while to master this," he said, glancing around. "Be aware of it and begin to think about what you want your lives to be. This is not wishful thinking, it's active dreaming. Realize that all your thoughts are connecting to the dream. Be clear about what you want." Roger was rapidly scribbling and the others were intently focused on taking in the words. "Later, in the Dreamtime Intensive, you will all have an opportunity to connect with your dream to make it real."

When the class ended, Steven told them to move to the courtyard for the closing ceremony. Martha checked her watch. It was almost four o'clock.

As they waited in the courtyard they discussed their new skills, wondering what they would do next and how soon they would see each other again. Angela told Martha she was planning to drop by.

"I'll watch for you," Martha said.

Soon the teachers arrived for the ceremony. Martha pulled Aurora Luna aside, explaining that she was supposed to be home in a few minutes. Then she told her about her son's phone call. Aurora pulled her into the office. "You can leave here after the closing ceremony, probably about nine, and still be home by four. I'll show you how it's done. However, it's an advanced technique. Please use it only this once for now. As for what your son said, it's unfortunate that anyone found out about the feather. It's not illegal, but it's definitely not something to advertise. Meet with this person but agree to nothing. Your best option may be to stall for a few more days. Trust that you'll know what to do."

Feeling less than confident, Martha thanked her and they went back outside.

Everyone gathered in a circle to say goodbye. "You have been awakened, all of you, to dormant powers," Aurora said. "Allow yourselves time to get used to these. Practice. Expect a few snafus. Maintain a sense of calm and a sense of humor. Share the energy. You will find people drawn to you. Speak only what is in your heart. Now, we are going to move through the portal to a sacred site not far from here." One by one they stepped into the portal and emerged a moment later in a field with a stone circle. Steven instructed everyone to gather sticks and branches for a fire. As Martha collected sticks, she sensed a lost part of herself emerging, one with an instinctive connection to the Earth. Her movements became fluid and graceful as she carted sticks back to the fire site. She looked around. Everyone, she saw, was moving this way, as if they were part of a ceremonial dance.

"You are experiencing connection," Aurora said, "with the Earth and with each other. We have forgotten how this feels, yet it is essential to life."

As she continued to look for sticks, Martha heard the trees making a deep sound, almost as if they were singing. A feeling of love and acceptance intensified inside her, like a joyous energy, until finally she no longer felt separate from the ground beneath her, the trees beside her, and the stars above her.

Soon the fire was blazing, creating both light and shadows as the sun went down. To Martha, everything seemed alive. A full moon rose. Olivia called them all close, and the fire warmed them as the night grew cool. "All of you contributed to this fire that is creating light and heat for us," she said. "Your energy and your intention were as essential as the trees who willingly dropped branches as offerings and the fire spirit whose breath made the blaze. We are at our most powerful when we collaborate creatively with other beings."

The three teachers' voices became a song that danced with the fire. Martha felt connected to something that was grand and encompassing yet also intrinsically a part of her. It spread inside her like the warmth from the fire. She felt complete. There was nothing missing in her life, and her loneliness had vanished.

The teachers called out, and a cloud of shimmering mothlike beings rose from the ground nearby. The students turned to watch. "Those are Clarifiers," Aurora said. "You can call on them for clarity in any situation. As Level 1s you have entered a world beyond the merely physical. Your ability to see and perceive and understand has changed. Thus, more will be revealed to you now by those who know you have the ability to see and understand them. It is important to be open and to practice. In the not too distant future when you return here you will be tested on your skills," she added. "We will see you all soon." With that they moved to the portal to return home.

10

Don't agree to anything, she reminded herself, coming in through the back door. At that moment there was a clap of thunder and it started to rain. She grabbed her umbrella, cut some flowers for the table, and quickly straightened the house. Then she put the quetzal feather in her desk drawer for safekeeping. At ten o'clock she pulled a small container from her overnight bag.

Inside was something Aurora had given her: a Keeper whose job was to keep the past. She released it in the living room as she had been instructed and it went to work, swooping around the house turning the clocks back to read four. She left her wristwatch set at ten, as Aurora had instructed. It was important that she herself stay oriented to the correct time context.

The front doorbell rang at once. She hurried to put the Keeper away, but she had a hard time catching it. The doorbell sounded again as she captured the creature and slipped it back in its container. If they escaped, Aurora warned her, they tended to reset clocks at random, setting them ahead or behind or stopping them altogether.

Clark stood on the porch with Henry Hocket. Henry had an envelope in his hand and she realized she still hadn't read the first packet he brought over. He greeted Martha as they came in. Showing her the envelope and then sticking it in his shirt pocket he told her that he had just learned it would soon be illegal to possess a quetzal feather. "I wanted to let you know as soon as possible. I think the smart thing is to avoid any potential problems. I told Clark I'd be happy to handle this for you, no questions asked." He assured her that he could work through channels to take care of everything. Martha weighed his words as he explained that the quetzals are nearly extinct and are protected as a result. She felt uncomfortable.

Henry shifted his weight. Hoping his plan would work he spoke carefully. "Unfortunately I am obligated to report this. If you like, you can turn the feather over to me and we can leave your name out of it. I'll take care of everything."

"Where did you get it, mom?" Clark interrupted. "I thought you got it in your Spanish class since you had it with you the other night. I didn't realize it was anything special."

He waited for her to answer, but Martha, remembering that Aurora had cautioned her about stalling for time, turned to Henry. "I appreciate your offer to help," she said. "However, I don't have it here at the moment. Perhaps I can call you later." She hoped her ruse would buy her some time.

"Sounds like a plan," Clark said, checking his watch. "I told Leslie I'd be home by five so I need to head that way. Why do you have all the lights on, mom?" The sun was streaming through the windows, and she had forgotten to turn the lights off.

Henry's eyes scanned the room and fell on the Level 1 certificate Martha had left on the table. He walked over to pick it up. "The Ancient Wisdom School," he said. "So you've been there?" He framed it as a question, but to Martha it sounded like an accusation. Clark had opened the door to leave.

Martha hadn't meant to leave the certificate out and she walked over to get it and put it in a drawer. Henry's stare was making her uneasy.

Henry didn't realize he was staring, but he had just confirmed that Martha knew more than she was saying. She was certainly not a typical student, he thought. He was surprised she was attending the school but it explained why she had the feather. And in spite of what she said, he sensed that she still had it. He would not give up.

Clark stood in the doorway. "I'll see you later, mom." Henry thanked her for her time and said if anything changed to call him.

Martha was thinking of what Aurora had said. *Emotion is a guide.* How was it guiding her? Why did she feel uneasy? All at once she remembered how late it was. She hoped she could get the clocks restored to the proper time when they were gone. She was quite sleepy.

Noticing her umbrella, Clark picked it up and put it away. "How'd this get wet?" he asked.

"It was raining when I got home," she said.

He frowned. "The sun's been out all day."

It was too late to correct her mistake. It was late and she was tired. "That's right," she said. "What was I thinking?"

Clark glanced at the professor and shook his head, implying that his mother was not always completely comprehensible.

When they were gone, Martha locked her door and pulled out the packet that Henry had given her earlier. Inside was an article he had written for a scientific journal detailing the quetzal's habits and habitat. She scanned it, looking for any information that might be useful. He also discussed the rich mythology surrounding the bird from the legends of ancient peoples. The feathers, he said, symbolized flying and higher consciousness; those who possessed a feather were believed to have access to such powers. The article included reproductions of two old paintings. The first showed the highly prized quetzal plumes, which looked like the leaves of a fern, being traded for a blanket. The second showed a costumed figure with an elaborate headdress of quetzal feathers. An odd sensation came over her as she realized that she had seen the original of the second painting at the school.

She took off her reading glasses and retrieved the feather from its hiding place. It looked like simply a beautiful feather. It was hard to believe it could bestow any special power. She wished it came with instructions.

She put it down and returned to the article. Henry went on to discuss the legend of Quetzalcoatl. There was speculation among some that the plumed serpent was entirely mythical and had never in fact existed, and it was this speculation that the professor hoped to prove wrong. He was in the process of translating ancient writings. However, except for the note about the powers attributed to the feathers, she found his article too dry to hold her interest.

At that instant she remembered that it was very late and she needed to reset her clocks. As she went to get the Keeper, her doorbell sounded. Ned stood at the door. "Found this in your yard," he said, handing her the envelope Henry had had in his shirt pocket.

"I'll see that he gets it," she replied.

"What's in the container?" He gestured at the Keeper.

"It's a long story," she said. "Can I tell you later?" She would have enjoyed talking with him, but Aurora had cautioned her against taking part in any interactions other than the one with Clark and Henry until she was more experienced. She promised to call him in the morning. Closing the door, she let the Keeper out. It quickly went to work, and with the clocks reset, Martha discovered that the rain had picked up and the wind was blowing ominously.

She didn't feel like sleeping but she settled into the comforting softness of her bed and pulled the covers up. It had been a long and eventful day and she certainly needed to rest. Yet something wouldn't let her. A moth flitted by the lamp on the nightstand, making a sound every time it touched the shade. Its insistence tugged at her.

She pulled on her fleece robe and went to look at the envelope Henry had dropped. It was postmarked Arizona. There was a reason this had come to her, she told herself. There was something she was supposed to know. But she stared at it for a minute before she was able to look inside. Finally reluctance gave way to curiosity. Perhaps it would help her to understand Henry's motivations.

Feeling like a spy, she carefully pulled the pages out and un-folded them. But she was spared from having to read them: they were blank.

It took her several minutes to calm herself after she discovered that Henry had lied. At first she was shocked, then angry. Then she realized she had to put her own interests first. But what was he up to? She wanted to find out and for a moment or two she wondered how she could.

He had mentioned a book of ancient writings about the quet-zal that he had in his office. She didn't know why, but she felt with certainty that she wanted to see it. Maybe it explained how to use the feather. She went to the closet for her raincoat, pulling it on over her nightgown. She didn't relish the idea of heading out in the storm, and she didn't know what was propelling her to pursue this, but a moment later she was standing outside. She had a new and unusual feeling that she was beginning to understand the force that was pushing her to act.

Briefly, she remembered Angela in England in her pink paja-mas and wondered if she should get dressed. But she wouldn't be using the portal, and she'd be back in just a few minutes. Her cell phone was in her pocket, just in case.

A gust of wind hit her, almost knocking her over. She pulled her raincoat tight and opened her umbrella. She was getting a mes-sage, and she decided she needed to act on it, even if it made no sense. She braced herself for the wind and rain as she leapt off her top porch step.

How the crow flies, the college was a mile away. Fortunately it was the same direction the wind was blowing because her flying skills were limited and she'd never flown at night. She made good time and managed to stop herself in some bushes by the building that housed science and art. She had not perfected landing and was glad no one was around as she disentangled herself from the brush. One of her slippers had fallen off and she retrieved it, but her um-brella was nowhere to be found.

The main doors to the building were locked. She poked around for a couple of minutes, wondering why she hadn't considered this possibility. It was insane to be out in such wild weather. The wind had intensified and was buffeting her. Leaves and debris flew as she covered her face. A sudden bolt of lightning lit up the darkness like an exclamatory warning from above, startling her. She ran to the side of the building to check for open windows. There had to be a way to get in. At that moment a massive tree cracked in a violent gust of wind. Timber shuddered as a large branch crashed downward. She barely got out of the way before it fell with tremendous force through the main doors.

She picked her way carefully over the glass and rubble and checked the directory inside. Then she hurried down a dark hall, coming to the office with Hocket's name on it. In the distance, she heard voices, evidently responding to the damaged doors. The wind howled, rattling the building. She tried the doorknob. Unbelievably, it turned in her hand. Someone had left it unlocked. Once inside, she quickly began to look around in the dark. There was a lamp on the desk. She switched it on and surveyed the small room. There was a shelf laden with books and journals. On top were two stuffed birds. Their beady eyes were fixed on her in an unnerving stare. Framed pictures of pyramids hung on the wall, and there were charts and notes everywhere. Behind the desk was a cabinet. She tried the doors; they were locked. The desk drawers were locked as well.

Without warning the office went dark. She froze, but then realized that the storm must have knocked the power out. Pulling a flashlight from her pocket she continued her search. Under some papers on the desk was a small book with a leather cover. It looked ancient. She held it in her hand, almost not wanting to open it. Slowly it dawned on her that she recognized it. It was the book the bird had given her in her dream. Perhaps, she thought, it held the secrets she was looking for.

The eerie connection with her dream made her mind spin. But before she could decide what to do, she heard voices in the hall. "I saw a light," a man said. "Do you have the key?" She had to do something. She tucked the book and flashlight in her pocket.

The office door opened. Two security guards came in, shining their flashlights around the room and under the desk. "Don't see anything," one of them said.

The next voice was familiar. "Was there any damage in here?" It was the professor, who had just arrived and was brushing rain off his jacket.

"Doesn't appear to be. We're checking the building. Thought we heard something." When they left he immediately opened the cabinet. In the darkness, Martha could not see inside. She hovered near the ceiling, reluctant to breathe in case he might hear her, but the wind was still blowing fiercely. He locked the cabinet, then prepared to leave. Almost as an afterthought he began looking for something else. He did not have a flashlight so after checking in a couple of places he left.

Martha floated down as carefully as she could, trying not to upend anything. She was amazed at what she had just done and wished she could tell Ned. Still trembling, she cautiously opened the door to leave. Henry was at the end of the hall, where a crew was cleaning up the mess. All at once he started back toward his office. Just as quickly, she turned and headed the other way.

"Who's there?" he called, seeing a shadowy form in the darkness. "Wait!"

She ran, wishing she had worn shoes instead of slippers. In fact, she wished she had taken the time to get dressed. She didn't relish being apprehended in her nightgown. She darted down a side hall and then up a flight of stairs. Out of breath, she looked around desperately for somewhere to hide. She heard his footsteps gaining on her.

She stepped through an open door and locked it behind her, praying he didn't have a key. She was in a chemistry lab. She moved toward the windows and opened one. Leaning out, her stomach fell away as she saw how far it was to the ground. She heard him trying a key in the lock. As the door opened, she grabbed a beaker of solution sitting at a workstation. As a last resort, she tossed it toward the door. It exploded when it hit the floor and she heard his cry of surprise as she jumped.

The storm kept Ned awake, and when it let up he went out to check the damage. He'd heard a tree go down in the street not far away. Sure enough, he found a large pine that had come down on a parked car, smashing the roof. The neighborhood was dark because the power was out, and he walked carefully to avoid any fallen lines. The ground was littered with leaves and branches, but the damp air was washed clean. Heading home, he saw a large object drop from the sky. He hurried to investigate, nearly tripping over Martha as she picked up her flashlight. She gave a startled squawk.

"Oh, I didn't know you were outside," he said. "I saw something flying. Was that you?"

"Come on in," she said.

"It's midnight," he reminded her.

"I can't talk out here." She started up her steps and he followed.

"I can come in for a minute. What's up?"

She unlocked her door and after they were both inside she explained where she had been. She lit some candles. He listened intently until she told him about the envelope with the blank pages. "You shouldn't have gone by yourself," he said. "I would have gone with you."

She showed him the book, and when he opened it and looked at the strange writing he asked her how she would read it. "It's just pictures and symbols," he said.

But as she leaned over to look at the page in the beam of light from his flashlight, the symbols came to life. It was as if she was standing in another world, and everything in it made sense to her.

11

Hocket stared out the window in disbelief. The person who had thrown the beaker had vanished into thin air. But with flames dancing across the floor, there wasn't time to waste. He raced from the room to report the fire. And with the security guards instructing him to get out of the building, he ran to check his office. He needed to save his notes, his files and most importantly, the book.

When he found it gone from the desk he was convinced he must have put it away, and he cursed the darkness. It was nearly impossible to find what he needed with a flashlight. He opened the desk drawers and searched the cabinet. In the distance he heard sirens approaching. With luck, the fire wouldn't spread. There wasn't time to get everything he needed without making several trips.

With a growing feeling of dread he carried an armload of paper to his car, but when he returned the fire marshal prevented him from going back into the building. He waited by his car, upset that he could lose all his work. By the time the fire was out, he had several nagging questions. Who had been in his office? And who was Martha and what did she know? According to her son, she'd never been more than a wife and a mother for years. It didn't add up. He asked the fire marshal how soon he could get back into the building, but he was told it might be several days. A crew was in the process of boarding it up until repairs could be made and its structural integrity determined.

For now, he had more questions than answers. When he had taken the job at the college in the small town, he considered it the middle of nowhere. Certainly it was too isolated and provincial to be useful in the long term. But for the time being, he found it gave him a great deal of freedom to pursue his research. Still, never would he have imagined it would be the one place on Earth where he would finally encounter an actual quetzal feather. What were the odds?

For many years the legend and history surrounding the bird had fascinated him. Finding the book was a coup. And the feather had fallen into his hands so easily it almost seemed fated. Somehow he would get it back. Then he would be able to conduct his experiments and determine what was true. He hadn't waited all these years to let an insignificant glitch stop him.

He had to act fast, though, because all of a sudden he remembered the umbrella. Why hadn't he thought about it sooner?

After Ned left, Martha sat down by candlelight to examine the book. It appeared to be a historical record of the quetzal and its powers. The pictures came to life as she looked at them, like videos, as if the energy stored in them for hundreds of years was released. Each tiny picture or glyph contained information, and she wondered why Ned couldn't see it. The bird was tied to the deity Quetzalcoatl, and she began to read the stories about how feathers had been given to a chosen few. There wasn't time to read it all, but as she turned the page, in one of the small pictures she saw the amulet that was now around her neck. She didn't understand all the references, especially to time, but the amulet had obviously been made ages ago. Why had it come to her? What was she supposed to do with it? The late hour made her sleepy. She decided to finish reading in the morning. Perhaps, too, she should visit Aurora to share this information. With so much on her mind, she thought she would never fall asleep, but she did, and slept without dreaming.

The morning newspaper carried a dramatic headline: Substantial Storm and Fire Damage at College. There was a front-page photo of the boarded-up science and art building, and she felt guilty as she read about the mysterious fire starter in the chemistry lab. Police were still investigating. Professor Hocket was unable to provide them with a description of the person he had seen fleeing the building. She felt relieved. Perhaps he hadn't recognized her.

She still couldn't believe her luck when she climbed out the window, closed her eyes, and jumped into the wind. She had landed safely in her own yard. Luckily, no one had seen her except for Ned. The building would be closed for several days, which gave her some needed time. She planned to return the book before he noticed it was missing, but first she wanted to finish reading it. She had gotten caught up in the legend of the bird from the cloud forest that had first shown up in her dream.

The quetzal, she learned, picking up where she left off the night before, was a transcendent creature with its feet in many worlds. Not limited by the usual dimensions of time and space, it could visit people when they were awake or dreaming. Its visionary powers allowed it to see beyond the physical world. Because it lived in treetops in remote areas, few people ever encountered it, and those who did were thought to become very powerful in their own right. The bird was considered sacred. When it took physical form it was so elusive that little was known of its habits. It seemed to appear and disappear without warning and was known for walking between the worlds. To her the information seemed so far-fetched it couldn't possibly be true.

She wondered where Henry had found the ancient book, and how much of it he had translated. It was obviously valuable because this was not a copy. The painted glyphs were original art, created by several artists, perhaps over many generations.

In the middle of the book she found what appeared to be a telling of a legend. There was once a great and gentle leader who had left for a new land called the Lost City. People had been searching for this place ever since, to no avail. She felt the hair stand up on the back of her neck as she thought of the city she had seen in her dream.

Still other glyphs showed the quetzal influencing the weather, turning clouds to sun and sun to snow. According to these accounts, it had made marshes into deserts and caused volcanoes to erupt. If the bird appeared, it was an omen of change. Very few feathers were found, but those who possessed one could accomplish feats unknown to other mortals.

As she turned the page to find out what those feats were, Martha discovered that a few pages of the book had been removed. Her mind raced. What did they describe? More importantly, where were they?

The phone rang, interrupting her thoughts. She answered, expecting it to be her son, but it was Henry, wondering if the storm had caused any problems at her house. She said that luckily it hadn't, but that she had seen in the paper the damage at the college.

"Yes, very unfortunate." He paused. Then he told her he was glad the quetzal feather was safe with her, that his office building had been the one damaged. He went on to say he had seen someone coming out of his office.

"I saw that in the paper," she said, relieved they were talking over the phone and not in person. "Was anything missing?"

"I couldn't see well in the dark," he said. "But I was unable to find a very rare book that I have." He paused, intending to let the silence grow so that it might incriminate her, but she stepped into it.

"I am sure you will find it when you are allowed to go back in your office. Were you told how long that will be?"

He said it might be several days. "Say, when I was there last night," he continued, "I noticed an umbrella outside the building." Something in his voice put her on edge.

"Do you think it's a clue?" she asked.

"I don't know," he said. "But it was a blue one with polka dots like yours. It made me think of you. Do you remember when Clark asked you about your umbrella and you said it had rained?"

She grew apprehensive. It was time to end his fishing trip, but before she could he said, "I didn't think much about it until it actually did rain later that night."

She was being pushed into a corner, and she needed time to think. "I'm a little forgetful," she said. "Sometimes I think it's Thursday when it's Friday."

He persisted. "I'm disappointed. I was hoping you were going to tell me you knew how to go forward and backward in time."

"If I could do that," she said with more confidence than she felt, "you would be talking to a much younger woman." Her comment broke the tension, and he laughed.

"You have a point." With that he switched gears. "If you need to contact me in the next few days, please feel free to call me at home."

She jotted down the number and hung up. She couldn't tell how much he knew, or if he simply had suspicions. Either way, she preferred to keep her distance from him for the time being.

Clark called a few minutes later. His office hadn't been damaged, but Matthew's birthday present was there, and now he couldn't get it. He said that all the locks at the building were being changed, because it appeared that someone had a key. "I guess I should be sure not to leave anything valuable in my office," he told her. She wanted to reassure him, but realized she couldn't. It would have to wait until after she returned the book, when everything could go back to normal. But then she thought about normal and realized she had no idea anymore what that meant. The normal world that she knew had given way to something quite unusual and unexpected.

Clark reminded her about Matthew's birthday. She had promised to bake him a cake. The whole family was coming for dinner later and she hadn't even begun the preparations. And even though she needed to contact Aurora as soon as possible, it would have to wait.

At that instant the doorbell rang. Tucking the book in her knitting bag, she went to answer and found a deliveryman wielding a large box. "Let me set it inside for you. Just sign here." He held up a metal clipboard.

She examined the label, which read to Chaco, 14 Owl Hill, Seaport. Under that were the words OPEN AT ONCE. Chaco, of course, was nowhere around and as she watched the delivery truck pull away, she wondered what to do.

All her life she had lived by such simple, understandable rules. One plus one equals two. A stitch in time saves nine. Don't burn the candle at both ends. In such a world, there is predictability. Nearly extinct birds don't show up out of the blue. Strangers don't know what you're thinking. And portals simply don't exist. But all at once everything was new and none of the old rules worked. And she had to decide what to do with a package addressed to a cat that said open at once.

After a few minutes of fretting and pacing, she heard a scratching sound. She moved closer to the box to listen, then cringed as a realization came over her: whatever was inside was alive.

She hurried to the door and called, but Chaco failed to materialize. So she examined the box from all sides. There were no holes for fresh air, which the creature must need to breathe. Taking care not to tip the box, she cut the tape and carefully opened the top just enough to peer in.

Later, when she remembered this incident, she would view it as the moment she lost control. It was the moment she realized that nothing was as it seemed. Reality was a direct consequence of perception. Like most people, she had seen what she wanted to see, and ignored the rest. She had viewed the portal as merely an adventure, and the school as a way to understand the experience.

Meanwhile, she had been catapulted from a routine and rather humdrum existence to literally living on the edge of reason and never knowing what would happen next. She had felt a semblance of control, but her mistake was to believe it. She pretended that nothing had really changed, and that there was no reason to use anything other than the ordinary caution that had served her all her life.

Yes, that was the watershed moment. As she peered in the box, a swarm of bugs emerged and flew into her face. She fell back, brushing them away, as thousands more began to buzz and flit around her living room. Soon they were everywhere in the house. Ladybugs clumped on the ceiling and an iridescent butterfly floated by. A swarm of bees found the roses in the living room. This was worse than a nightmare, she thought, opening doors and windows as fast as she could. This took some time, and she noticed some of the bugs were simply flying out one window and in another. Finally the large butterfly moved out into the garden, and before she could wonder what her son would think about it, an iguana, which was sunning itself on a rock in the garden, ate it.

She wasn't sure where the iguana had come from. There were no iguanas in this part of the world. The box! She had never looked inside it to see if it was empty.

There was only one item left in it—a string of Japanese lanterns. Thinking they would be festive for the party, Martha headed to the garden with them, brushing a moth aside as she went. No sooner was she outside than Ned arrived.

"You'll need a ladder," he said, and off he went. "She's in the back," she heard him say as he rounded the corner, and a few seconds later the excited voices of her grandchildren surrounded her.

"Mom, you need to close the windows." It was Clark. "You're letting all kinds of bugs in the house." She handed him the string of lanterns.

"Make yourself useful," she instructed, hoping all the bugs would fly out before she went to bed. The children went to look for Chaco. Ned returned, carting a ladder with his brother-in-law at the other end. Joe looked as if he had been pulled away from doing something more important, like watching a televised baseball game. But he chipped in, and the lanterns were hung in no time. Everyone stood back to admire their handiwork, and the children clamored for them to be turned on. "They come on automatically as soon as it's dark enough," Martha said, reading the instructions. "It looks like all we can do is wait."

Clark ordered a pizza for dinner. "Leslie will be here soon," he said. "I told her to pick up a cake on her way over."

"Chocolate," Matthew said.

"Strawberry," Melissa pleaded.

"It's my birthday. I get to choose."

"Strawberry on your birthday, Melissa," Clark said. "No fighting."

Martha invited Ned and Joe to join the festivities. They accepted eagerly, since Carol was away for a day and this meant they didn't have to eat leftovers. Ned looked quite happy. She went to toss a salad. Matthew, who had added turnips to his juggling routine and was juggling like a pro, entertained everyone. He and Melissa had begun to eat many new fruits and vegetables, and he told his grandmother what turnips tasted like. "I don't need to eat those again," he added, turning up his nose.

Angela appeared a short time later, and Martha invited her to dinner as well. "The more, the merrier," Martha said, then leaned close to whisper. "I'm so glad you're here. I need your help. How is everything going?"

"Well, I got here," Angela said. "I made one wrong turn and ended up in the middle of an outdoor wedding on a beach. I wasn't concentrating. That's my challenge and I'm working on it. But I found this beautiful sand dollar."

"Way cool," Matthew said, coming over to admire it.

"It's yours," Angela told him.

"Dad, look!" He ran over to his father with the shell.

"What's up?" Angela asked, waving some flies away. "You have a lot of flies. Maybe we should eat inside."

"Trust me. It's better out here," Martha told her. Melissa tugged on her arm. "What is it, dear?"

She handed her grandmother a small smooth stone. "Chaco gave it to me,"

"Then I'm sure he'd want you to keep it."

"No, it's for you. To solve your puzzle." She scampered off.

Martha stared at the stone in her palm and wondered how it could help her solve the problem she was facing. Not having a clue, she tucked it in her pocket.

After Matthew opened his presents they all sat down to their picnic feast, eating by candlelight so that they could keep an eye on the lights. The children could barely contain their excitement. As everyone sang "Happy Birthday," the lanterns in the garden came on, filling the darkness with a festive glow. "Look!" Melissa exclaimed again and again, pointing at each new light. It was as if a sea of stars had settled in the yard of 14 Owl Hill. They shone from the trees and the bushes and even the rainforest vine, tiny lights sparkling like bright jewels. A hush fell over the table.

"What are those flashing lights?" Matthew asked.

"Well, I'll be," Ned said. "I haven't seen a lightning bug in years."

A feeling of happiness spread through the gathering. Clark looked at his children and smiled with affection and pride, then reached out and held both of their hands. Martha was having so much fun she had almost forgotten about her conversation with Henry.

"This was a good party," said Joe, setting his napkin on the table.

"I second that." Ned smiled. "It was a great party. I hope we can do it again."

"I think he likes you," Angela said after everyone left.

"We don't have time to think about that," Martha said, telling Angela what had happened, ending with the missing pages. "I need to find them."

"You think they describe what powers the feathers have?"

"Yes," she said. "That's what I'm hoping."

"And you think the professor has them?"

"Maybe. I want to have another look around his office. Something tells me he's up to no good."

"You can't just break in."

Martha eyed her conspiratorially.

"Wait, you want me to help?"

"What if he discovers I have the book? I need to do something before he does."

Angela thought for a minute. "You have a point. But—"

Chaco came over and sat by their feet. *Use the stone,* he said.

"He's a Level 3," Martha explained. "If we could only talk to him. Oh!" She pulled the stone out of her pocket. "This is supposed to help." She handed it to Angela, who put it first in one palm and then the other.

The stone will help you.

Angela turned the stone over in her hand. "I don't know," she said. "The thing about being a beginner is trying to figure this stuff out."

"I've been using trial and error," Martha said, "but it's a little hair-raising."

Chaco stared at them. *¡Caramba! Use your intuition. That's why you have it.*

Angela laughed. "I have an idea. We'll make a chart of our options. Then we'll toss the stone in the air and see where it lands. It might seem haphazard but you never know." They went to work and were ready in a few minutes. They spread the chart, made from several pieces of paper taped together, on the floor. Then Angela handed Martha the stone. "You should throw it. It's your dilemma."

Chaco watched them, but he was losing patience. How long was this going to take? This challenged even his Level 3 skills.

Martha tossed the stone into the air above their chart. It fell and bounced off the paper. Angela told her to try again. This time it bounced once and split open. Out tumbled a tiny key. "Oh!" they exclaimed in unison.

"What does it unlock?" Martha asked.

Trust yourself. Move in the direction of what you are looking for, even if you don't have all the answers. Chaco walked across the chart and sat down in the middle, trying to get their attention. *Time is wasting.*

It took them a full minute before they noticed where the stone had landed—in the circle marked "break into office."

Angela helped clean up the dishes as Martha fretted about what they were going to do. "I already did it once. Twice seems over the top," she said.

"But he lied about the feather," Angela reminded her. "Who knows what he planned to do with it. You need to find the missing pages so you know what the feather can do. I think that's what Aurora would tell you."

"If we have a key, it's not really breaking in," Martha reasoned. She thought for a moment. "But they may have more security there because of the fire."

"In this small town? I doubt it. Now, how should we get there and what should we wear?" Angela quickly changed gears, because she wanted to look good. "I suggest dark clothes to make us less visible, like in the movies," she added. They headed for Martha's closet, tittering with anticipation.

¡Ay-yay-yay! Chaco hunkered down on the couch. Enough was enough. Even though he could hear them talking, he closed his eyes for a short nap.

"I'm sure my friends think I'm climbing into bed about now with a good book," Martha said, pulling out a dark sweatshirt. "I almost can't remember what my life was like before all this started."

"Do you want to?"

"You have a point, dear. It was boring…and a bit lonely. I was wondering what I was going to do with all the spare time on my hands." She laughed. "I haven't had a spare moment since all this started."

"How many people get an opportunity like this?" Angela asked, choosing a black sweater. "Drat, I almost broke a nail."

Martha wondered how she would ever work in the garden with fingernails as long as Angela's. "I wonder if this is the chance of a lifetime or...." Her voice trailed off.

"Or what?" Angela asked as they headed downstairs.

"That's what I don't know," Martha said, deciding to keep her uncertainty to herself.

Angela grabbed Murray's baseball hat off the hook in the hall. "This is perfect. I don't want my hair to get messed up. Do you mind?"

For a moment, she did. But then she swore she heard Murray say, *Go for it, kiddo.* She tucked the key in her pocket.

"Do you have any gum? It helps when I'm nervous."

Martha searched in her purse and found a stick of Dentyne.

"No Juicy Fruit?" Angela unwrapped it and hurried to catch up. Martha was already out in the driveway, hovering.

"Shall we fly?"

"This is gonna be great. Show me how you do it." But they were interrupted by a voice and turned to see a dark figure heading up the drive. They were relieved to discover it was only Ned, out for a walk.

"Where are you two off to?"

Martha settled back on the ground. "We were getting a little fresh air."

"Same here. Just saw a couple of your lightning bugs. Are you sure you're not going for ice cream? I could give you a lift."

She thought for a moment. "You could give us a lift to the college," she said, thinking that might be a wiser idea than testing Angela's novice flying skills. "Angela is interested in seeing it."

"Hop in the car," he said. "I would love to escort you. It sounds like an adventure. Shall I get a flashlight? It might be hard to see at night." He disappeared into the house on his errand.

"We can't take him," Angela said.

"He can wait in the car."

Angela stuck her lower lip out. "I wanted to fly."

"Now might not be the time to learn," Martha told her. "Remember our portal tour. We're pressed for time here."

Ned returned and they set off. It took them only a few minutes to get there. "Sure you don't want company?" he asked, pulling up as Martha instructed near the science and art building and shutting off the engine.

"If you stay in the car you can park in this No Parking zone," Martha said. "That way you're close." He agreed it made sense and handed over the flashlight. "We won't be long." She and Angela cut across the sidewalk from the student union, walking quickly until they were out of view. Martha led the way to their destination and shone the light on the boarded-up doors. The building was posted No Admittance. "Let's try the back," she said. Sure enough, the key worked, letting them inside the dark building. "This way. I hope the security guard isn't around," she whispered. After a moment they found Hocket's office and discovered the small key worked again. Martha approached the locked cabinet while Angela held the light. Again she tried the key. Again it worked, and she opened the doors.

12

For some reason, Martha had expected to find answers. But as she rummaged through several items, all she had was questions. "I don't see anything that looks like the missing pages. But I don't know how I would find them anyway. They could be hidden anywhere."

"Are you sure they're not here?" Angela swept the light over all the shelves of the cabinet.

"He checked this cabinet for something when I was here. It was too dark to see what he was looking for." She stared at an empty spot on the top shelf. "He may have taken something," she finally said.

Angela began checking the rest of the office, swinging the beam of the flashlight around through the shadows.

"He knows those pages are valuable," Martha said. "Of course, perhaps they weren't in the book when he got it." She hadn't considered that possibility before, and it stopped her in her tracks. Maybe she and Angela were on a wild goose chase.

"Where would you hide a couple pages?"

"Anywhere. In another book. We can't keep Ned waiting."

Angela checked the bookshelf, reaching behind some of the books. Without meaning to, she bumped one of the stuffed birds, and it tumbled down with a thud. Martha, who was already skittish, jumped out of the way, only half-stifling a cry of surprise. Angela stared with dismay at the up-ended mallard on the floor. "I'm not going to touch it," she said, backing away. "No way."

"You can't leave it there."

"I swear I am absolutely not touching it." She sounded on the verge of hysteria.

Martha didn't relish touching it either, but she finally reached down to get it while Angela held the light. Gingerly she picked it up by one leg, which came off in her hand. The bird bounced on the floor and the metal band around its ankle clinked on the floor and rolled under the desk. "Now look what you've done," Martha said.

"I didn't do it," Angela said, swearing in disbelief. Then she started to giggle as Martha tried to prop the bird back in its original position on the shelf. It sat there a moment, then tipped to one side like a moored boat at low tide.

"This will never do," she said with a sense of urgency. "Find the band while I look for some glue."

Angela reluctantly got down on the floor and shone the light under the desk. "I can't see it." Tension was building as they realized this was taking longer than they had planned, and they were both growing edgy.

Martha located some tape in the desk drawer. "It will show," she said. "But maybe he'll think the custodian did it."

"I almost broke another nail," Angela said, standing up and brushing off her jeans. "Wait, I have an idea. Use my gum." She pulled it out of her mouth.

"What?" Martha was beginning to lose patience with the situation. She stared at Angela in disbelief.

"It's worth a try. I fixed a hem in my skirt once that way."

Disgusted, Martha took it from her. "If I'm going to touch your chewed gum and a dead duck, then you have to find that band!"

Angela could tell she meant it. She crawled under the desk again with the flashlight. The space was tight, and she made a couple of grunting sounds, as if she were trying to get into a position to see. "Ow!" she cried, banging her head as she stood up. "There."

She thrust the band at Martha, who soon had the bird looking almost good as new. When she placed it on the shelf, they admired her handiwork. "You can't even tell," she said. "Gum. Who'd have thought? Now let's get out of here."

She shone the light at Angela. "What's that on your hat?"

Angela screeched. Expecting it to be a spider, she tore the hat off and threw it down, then shook her hair.

Martha reached for the hat. "An envelope. How odd." It was stuck to the back of the baseball cap.

"Maybe when I hit my head…"

Since it wasn't sealed, Martha opened it while Angela held the light. "The missing pages," she exclaimed. "I can't believe it. Good work." Martha suddenly felt uneasy. "Quick," she said, as a creepy-crawly sensation came over her. "We need to leave. Someone's coming."

No sooner had they closed the office door than they heard footsteps. Martha grabbed Angela's arm and they ran. A moment later they pushed through the doors into the night air. Across the way they saw the car, and as they hurried toward it Ned climbed out to open the doors. Martha glanced back over her shoulder as she got in but saw no one. She hoped they hadn't been spotted.

"That didn't take you long," Ned said as they got in. "Everything OK?" He cast Martha a questioning glance. She nodded, too winded to speak. "You didn't have to hurry on my account," he added.

"We're ready when you are," Angela said, hoping to dispense with the pleasantries in case someone was on their trail. In her haste to climb in the car, she upended a bag of donation items Joe had put in the backseat. She righted the bag and began piling things back in—a purse, golf shoes, a coffee mug, a small stuffed toy that looked like an extraterrestrial.

"I had a chat with that fellow I met at your house," Ned said, starting the car. "Did you see enough or do you want to go around the block?"

"We're set," said Angela, positioning the toy alien on the back-seat as Martha checked with her to make sure the pages were safe.

"What do you mean?" Martha was still edgy from what they had done.

"The professor. He was surprised you were wandering around so late. Went to look for you. I pointed him in the wrong direction." Angela glanced behind them one more time and saw someone running from the science and art building. She tapped Martha's shoulder and pointed.

With a sinking feeling, Martha stared at the dark figure. "So you told him we were here?"

"He put two and two together," Ned said. "He asked me if I'd seen that quetzal feather you have."

Martha felt the color drain from her cheeks. She wondered why Henry was at the campus so late. The dark figure she had seen had disappeared. Something moved in the shadows but she couldn't make out what it was. The light changed and Ned pulled onto the nearly deserted main road.

"Wait. You're going the wrong way," she said. She had been too distracted to give him directions. Ned looked for a place to turn around, but there weren't even any driveways. They were headed out of town. Angela was nervously monitoring the road behind them. She sank down in the seat as a car appeared and began to gain on them. Its headlights lit up the interior of the car.

"What did you tell him about the feather?"

"I told him I saw it a few days ago, which was true, but not since then. We didn't chat too long after that. He went to look for you."

The car had pulled up close behind them, and the glare of the headlights reflected in the rearview mirror. Squinting, Ned reached up to adjust it so he could see. "Someone's in an all-fired hurry," he said. Angela felt her heart pounding. What if it was Henry and he knew they'd been in his office? What if he knew they had pocketed the hidden pages? She pulled the hat lower on her head.

"Perhaps we should let that car go around," Martha suggested, looking down a precipitous embankment to the river.

"If I saw a good place to pull off, I would." Ned had a tight grip on the wheel and was driving with a seesaw motion that suggested his growing tension. He had picked up speed. The road followed the river and when he took a curve it felt like the car almost left the pavement. Angela hunkered down with her knees braced against the back of the front seat. Martha suddenly realized she had forgotten to fasten her seatbelt and she reached for it.

An oncoming car appeared around a curve and Martha, blinded by its lights, held on to the dash. The countryside was dark and there was no moon. An animal scurried off the road just in front of them and Ned swerved.

"Oh my God," Angela muttered, gripping the seat for dear life.

Martha wracked her brain for something she had learned at the Ancient Wisdom School that would serve her now. Oh for a portal you could drive a car into.

When the car left the road, she braced herself for the steep embankment, the tearing sound of trees and metal, the breaking glass, the cold water of the river. Angela screamed as branches snapped and leaves slapped the windows. After that, there was eerie silence as they plummeted through the air. The silence surprised Martha. She focused on it, following it in her mind to some far-off place. She waited for the impact.

The sound of Ned's voice was so hollow it surprised her. "What's going on?"

She was still holding the dashboard. She had never gotten her seatbelt fastened. "What do you mean?"

"Look out there." His voice was very small, as if it had been compressed to the size of a pea.

Martha looked but couldn't see anything. Not until she leaned toward the window could she see what he meant. The ground was quite some distance below them.

"Don't move," Ned said. "Don't even breathe. We must be stuck in the top of a tree."

"I don't think so," said Martha. "We're still moving." Far below, she could see the lights of a farmhouse. Angela carefully inched up in the seat and peered out.

Then she erupted with excitement. "We're flying! It's my dream come true!"

"If I can remind you," Ned said slowly, still holding the steering wheel as if he were driving, "we're in a car. To the best of my knowledge, cars don't fly."

"They evidently do now," Angela said, smiling happily at the stuffed extraterrestrial next to her, which looked very much at home in its pseudo-spaceship.

Martha was not sure why they were flying, and she certainly didn't want to make any sudden movements. Remembering her experiences of trying to land, she felt somewhat apprehensive. However, the feeling of being high in the night sky was exhilarating. "Cut the motor," she said.

Ned did as instructed and the silence encompassed them. It was majestic. They floated like a puff of willow seed. The stars spread out in a galaxy around them and a sliver of moon rose on the horizon.

"If this doesn't beat all," Ned said after a time. "I wish Carol could see this." He reconsidered for a moment. "Well, maybe not. Don't think she'd be too happy since this is her car. In fact, it would probably give her apoplexy." He was rambling, and Martha, touching the amulet around her neck, quieted him.

As far as she could tell, they were flying only because she thought about it. And she was very glad she had, in the nick of time, thought of something. Who knows what would have happened if…. She stopped herself. They were fine. That's what was important. She needed to focus on the next step, landing. She wouldn't do what she had done last time she flew, which was think about crashing into the bushes to stop herself. She would picture landing somewhere sensible. Her mind went to work. Her first choice was her own street but that was too risky. Ignoring the commentary from Ned and Angela, she pictured other possibilities. Of course, the high school! It had a parking lot that was empty at this time of night. As she thought about it the car turned and began to head toward the lights of town in the distance. It wouldn't take long.

Meanwhile, Ned was beginning to enjoy himself. "This must be what gliders are like," he said, to no one in particular. "Quiet. It's like being a bird. Am I steering, or is somebody else? Why is the car turning?" he asked.

"We're headed to the high school to land," she said.

He seemed disappointed that their flight would end, but he understood. "I'll just keep doing what I'm doing. Let me know if I should drop the landing gear." He chuckled. "Have you done this before?"

When she shook her head, he took a tighter grip of the wheel. "Carol would absolutely kill me if she knew," he said. "Mum's the word."

At that moment his cell phone rang. "Oh, no. It's Carol. What do I do?"

"Answer it."

"But what do I say?"

"You'll think of something."

Reluctantly he took one hand off the steering wheel to answer. "Hello... Yes, I know. I gave Martha and Angela a ride to the college...." There was a long pause. "They wanted to see it.... No, we're headed home now." Another pause. "What's that? I couldn't hear you.... You're kidding." He looked toward Martha and raised his eyebrows. "A UFO? Whereabouts?" He shook his head as he put the phone back on the dash. "She said, be careful. There was a UFO sighting."

As they neared the school, they noticed a line of cars and pickups headed that way. There were two police cars with their lights flashing and sirens wailing.

"I wonder what happened," Ned said. "Guess we have a birds-eye view." He scanned the ground below.

"Turn on the radio," Martha suggested. "It's something big."

Ned tried a couple of stations and finally found some news. "...We've been tracking it for some time. It was hovering outside of town and now it's headed to the high school. Somebody said it looks like it's going to land."

Realization dawned as Martha stared at the growing crowd. "They're talking about us," she said with dismay. "Evidently they can see us. We need a new plan."

"They think we're a UFO?" Angela said. "Oh, great. What if they shoot at us?"

Not far beneath them, more cars pulled up and people milled around, pointing.

"The headlights. We never turned them off." Martha's alarm prompted Ned and he quickly shut them off. "We have to get out of here."

"We won't be able to see without the lights," he said.

"What is way more important right now," Angela noted, "is they won't be able to see us."

"We need altitude," Ned said as the car continued to descend. "And fast. Would it help if I started the motor?" They were still several hundred feet up.

"No. Now hush. I'm trying to focus." Martha remembered what had happened when she flew with Ned over the river. She didn't relish the idea of plummeting to the ground in a car. Ned turned the steering wheel this way and that to no avail while she visualized the park about two miles away. Angela surveyed the scene below. Her window was halfway down, and on impulse she dropped the stuffed extraterrestrial into the crowd.

As the car began to gain altitude and pick up speed, people jumped in their vehicles, hoping to follow. In the commotion, a traffic jam ensued with lots of honking and shouting. With its headlights off, the silver car quickly vanished into the night.

"Does that count as my lesson?" Ned asked as he pulled in the driveway. "I hope not, because I still don't know how you do it." He'd been quiet on the drive from the park to the house, patiently listening to Angela chatter with relief and excitement.

"Come over first thing in the morning," she told him. "We'll talk then." For the moment, she was too tired to do much more than make her way into the house.

"Did you know you left a window open?" Angela asked, coming up the walk.

Martha frowned, because she thought she had closed them all after her episode with the box of bugs, but evidently she hadn't. "I hope my forgetfulness means my bug zoo has all flown out," she said.

As soon as they were inside Angela pulled out the manuscript pages. Given everything that had happened Martha had forgotten about them. "I'll read them to you," said Angela, trying to decipher the glyphs.

Martha settled into a chair, closing her eyes to ponder the last two days. They seemed like a whirlwind. Here she was, living a life she could not have imagined a few weeks ago—attending school in Mexico, hop-skipping around the world, and flying, of all things. Every bit of it surprised her, but she was actually growing accustomed to the unexpected turns and twists. In the beginning it boggled her mind and left her feeling as if she didn't understand. Lately, it seemed she was more adept at going with the flow. She was learning to trust herself, and to trust the feelings she had. She was still uncertain of the outcome, but she was much more comfortable with the process. She was also growing more familiar with her new skills. She knew it would take her a while to master them, but at least she was using them with more competence and even sharing them with others. But there was so much to learn! The feather, for instance—what was she was supposed to do with it?

"'I think I've got this," Angela began, triggered by the unspoken question. "I'm using my intuition. It looks like there are three primary powers. The first one is weather-shifting."

"Do you mean changing the weather?" Martha asked.

Angela cocked her head. "The second one is shape-shifting."

"That was in the article," Martha said. "The ability to change form."

"The third one is—" She struggled to decipher the words. "I can't really tell what it says. Something about the future. Can you make it out?" She handed the page to Martha, but even she had trouble with it.

Chaco, stretched out on the back of the couch, sat up and looked at them. *Each power in its own time. Es muy importante. When you can read the words, the power is available to you.*

"Maybe it's seeing the future. I can't tell either."

"We need to talk with Aurora. But wait, there's more." She leaned over Martha's shoulder, reading. "The quetzal gives the feather in invitation. It is given to those who will walk the great road. I wonder what that means."

"I don't know, but Henry wasn't given a feather. So maybe he can't read what's in these pages."

"Maybe. But he is definitely going to be looking for them if he finds out they're missing. He may come here. Have you thought of that?"

"I want to return them before he notices they are gone." Martha retrieved the book and put the missing pages back in. Then she stuck it back in her knitting bag.

"Do you think that was him behind us tonight in the car?"

"I couldn't tell. But if it was, he must think we're at the bottom of the river with his pages."

"You're right. The last time he saw us, we were plunging down the embankment. And if he went to his office and checked, he knows something is up." Angela looked as if she was scheming about something. "Where is the feather?" she asked. "I think we should experiment a little bit."

"It's not a toy," Martha said. "It's been given to me for a reason. I have to learn how to use it."

"Just show it to me. I've never even seen it."

After Angela agreed not to try anything, Martha said she would show it to her. She went to get it from the drawer where she had put it for safekeeping. The drawer was open, and she stared at it for several seconds before it finally registered with her that the feather was gone.

It was midnight when Angela left, and Martha slept fitfully. She had the sheet pulled over her head, but through it she could still see the phosphorescent glow of lightning bugs flashing on and off. A few moths flitted here and there. Fortunately, most of the bees had gone outside earlier when she'd opened the windows, and the few that were left settled down when she turned off the lights.

She was worried about the feather. She was also certain she hadn't left the window to the den open when she'd gone to the college with Angela. The logical explanation was that someone had been in her house, and she sensed it was Henry.

During the night she had a dream about the quetzal. This time she was in her garden when she noticed it standing off to the side. As soon as she saw it, it spoke. "You are being called," it said, "to be who you are, not who you were." When the bird flew off, she turned into a jaguar and began to dance. She woke with a start. Try as she might, the meaning escaped her.

Ned was sitting on the front porch reading the paper when Martha opened the door. "You're an early bird," she said.

"Hardly slept a wink," he replied. "Look at the headline." He held the paper up for her to see as he read it aloud. "UFO Spotted Over Seaport." There was a grainy photo. "All my life I wanted to see a UFO and now I am one. Not sure how I feel about that. Thank goodness," he whispered, "that Carol can't tell that it's her car."

"Why don't you come in?" she said. "I'm just brewing some tea and I'll pour you a cup." He followed her into the kitchen.

"I want to apologize," he began. "That mess last night was my fault. I can't tell you how relieved I am that you were able to save the day. But you have to admit that this whole business challenges the mind. It's not a part of my experience, to be sure, so I think it's impossible. But I can't argue with what happened."

She nodded. "It does seem impossible. I never would have believed it until it happened to me."

He sipped his tea. "I'll have to get some of this," he said. "Where do you buy it?"

She shook her head, telling him it was a gift.

"Do you have any idea how the flying happens?"

"I don't," she said. "All I know is it has to do with the fact that we accept more limitations than we need to, some of them in the name of science. Maybe you should think about going to the school."

"That is the craziest idea I ever heard," he replied, falling silent. Chaco walked into the room and gave her a look as if he thought it was crazy too.

"I've never met anyone like you," Ned finally said. "There's something intriguing about you, something irresistible."

"Aurora told me about that," she said. "The energy is irresistible, once you embrace who you are and begin to live from that authenticity."

"Tell me about Aurora."

Martha admitted she didn't know that much about Aurora except that she had studied the lost arts for many years with her mother and her grandfather. "When we're at the school, we spend most of our time in class. There's a lot to learn, and that's what we focus on. The details of a person's life—like what they do or where they're from—seem insignificant. I still don't know what Angela does for a living, for instance."

Before she could finish, the doorbell interrupted them. It was Carol. "There you are. I've been looking for you everywhere. I thought maybe you'd been abducted."

"Just having some tea," he said. "Got up early and didn't want to wake you. I noticed Martha was up."

"You left the door unlocked." Carol seemed more agitated than usual. "I don't feel safe after those aliens were around last night."

"Will you join us for tea?" Martha offered.

"No thanks. I just had coffee." She turned to Ned again. "There are leaves and twigs on the bumper of the car and stuck in the grille. Joe's going to wash the car. Where in the world did you go? I hope you weren't trying to find that spaceship." She picked up the paper and looked at the photo again. "I never thought we'd see one here."

Ned mumbled something about running over a branch in the road.

"Well, if you can free up some time, Joe could use a hand. He wants to go golfing. I told him I hoped he could get the windows done first."

"I'm on my way," Ned said. He followed Carol to the door. As Carol headed home Ned turned to Martha and flapped his arms. "See you later," he said with a wink.

13

A rooster crowed in the City of Eternal Spring as day broke, and a motorbike purred by in the street. Martha sipped her Celestial Citrus, greeting other students as they arrived. She hadn't gotten a chance to talk to Ned before she left, as he'd gone to the golf course with Joe. She felt happy to be back at the school. It was more familiar this time, and she was looking forward to the Level 2 classes, wondering what she would learn during this session.

Everyone was anticipating the first Level 2 class—even Roger, who brought Milky Ways for everyone. "I've got it down," he told Steven. "Let me know if you're hungry."

"I'd like *huevos rancheros*," Steven said, nibbling on papaya.

Roger grinned. "That must be Level 2. I hope I'm up to it."

Nobody came by public transportation this time. They had all mastered portals and had stories to share about their mistakes, especially Roger, who ended up in his neighbor's living room. "Not enough speed," Aurora said. "You can't be timid."

After breakfast they filed into Power Arts, reputed to be one of the more challenging classes. "We know you've all worked hard since your Level 1 experience," Steven said, congratulating them as they grew quiet. "You've learned in the best manner possible, by trusting yourself and trusting your own knowing. There is trial and error involved because you are learning to trust yourself. How many of you find you are hesitant to do that?"

Hands shot up around the room. "I'm never sure it's going to work," Roger admitted.

"Eventually you'll accept that it does," Steven noted, continuing with a tone of reassurance. "But there's a reason you're finding it challenging. This information goes counter to every rule you have lived by up to this point." His gaze scanned the room. "How many of you have realized that the rules you grew up with have quit working?" Again there was a show of hands. "How many of you feel the rules you live by run counter to some internal truth?" Martha nodded with the others in affirmation.

"When you live by all the rules you've been taught and all the beliefs you've been given," Steven continued, "you assume you will live happily ever after. The rules should work, but they don't. Does anyone know why?" When there were no ideas, he went on, speaking slowly to give each word emphasis. "You were taught to give your power to someone else. Let me tell you something." His eyes swept the room as his tempo picked up. "If you don't own your power," he said, pointing a finger at his chest, "then someone else does. If you're not using it"—he pointed out at the class—"someone else is. Think about it. How many times do you ask other people to make your decisions? Or agree with them that they can? How many times do you accept a belief unchallenged? How many of your own beliefs that you live by have you examined? How many times do you go against yourself?" Again he surveyed the room as brows furrowed. "These are the ways we give our power to other people and to the culture of our conditioning." He paused for a moment to let everyone catch up.

"Beginning now, you will live from your power center." He made a sweeping gesture with his arm and a wave of energy passed through the room. There were small sounds as if students had been punched in the gut. Everyone sat up straight as if they had come to life. "Did you feel that? That is your power center." Angela held her midsection with both hands as Steven went on to explain that their power center was the impetus of all action. "It is the part of you that you have let languish. It has nothing to do with control, nothing to do with controlling other people. It is about living fully. It will bring you completely to life."

Martha felt like she was on fire. She thought she was going to have to stand up and dance, or at the very least run around the room.

"I know you feel like moving," Steven said. "I am going to ask you simply to sit still and focus on your power and what it feels like. There will be time to move later." He gave them a few minutes to feel what was happening in them. Roger was having trouble sitting still. Steven walked over and put a hand on his shoulder and Roger grew calm. "It probably feels foreign to you," he said. "Unfamiliar. Perhaps unsettling. Get to know it. You will be learning to live with this feeling. Soon it will be completely natural. Do you know people who have everything and still say something is missing? It's their power center. When you connect to this, nothing is missing in your life."

As Steven walked around the room, his voice seemed to permeate to the very core of their being. "You will learn to live from your power center. It will bring you to living with balance. It will lead to nonreactive response. In other words, when something happens, you will respond rather than react. What you do will be active rather than passive. It will be a choice made with awareness."

"Can you give us an example?" Roger asked.

"Let's say someone takes a parking spot that you finally found. You get angry. That's a reaction." His voice grew quieter. "A response is to create another parking spot. Because your intention is to park, not to spend part of your day angry at a stranger."

They spent the rest of the class doing exercises to strengthen their power center. "Begin to use it for every action," Steven said, "so that it will become part of your being."

Martha had wondered how she would remember everything she learned at the school, but it stayed with her. It seemed to imprint on her essence with a new pattern of behavior. She told Angela she felt like it had always been there, and she was just waking up to it. The experiences were the most real she'd ever had. She was discovering a self that had been hidden away while she met the expectations of her various roles. It was springing to life like a seed, sprinkled with the water of awareness. She felt vibrant and focused, as if she had been realigned and was seeing everything from a new perspective.

"Martha?"

Steven's voice brought her back to her surroundings.

"I see you've connected with who you are."

"Yes," she said. "It's very new. I'm not used to it yet. I'm just enjoying the sensation."

"It will take a while to get to know who you are," he told her. "Stay with the feeling of newness. It will come to be familiar."

"I feel that way, too," Roger said.

"You will all experience this," Steven explained, moving effortlessly around the room as he talked. "The expansion of your true self is taking place. Once you become who you truly are you will experience a joy of recognition. The joy will bubble inside you like an underground spring and as it seeks a way out it may make you gleeful for no reason. Your glee may be contagious. Others may get caught up in it.

"For now, know that you have connected to your power centers. Later you will connect your power centers to the source." A murmur went around the room. They had heard about this, but none of them knew what the experience or sensation would be.

After class Aurora pulled Martha aside. "I imagine you have noticed your skills are outpacing your training," she said, motioning for her to take a seat in the shade by the fountain. "You seem to be handling this well."

"Thank you, but I don't seem to have much choice." As soon as she spoke, she realized she had taken the passive position, and she tried to decide how to change it. "What I meant was, I've noticed this too and I have been trusting myself to know what to do."

Aurora searched her face. "You've been unusual from the start. This is why you were entrusted with the amulet. It is why the quetzal empowered you with a feather. Tonight," she continued, "you will do the Dance of the Jaguar."

Martha's jaw dropped. She had just dreamed about this. "I'm not really much of a dancer."

"You must stop qualifying things," Aurora stated. "Women tend to do this. It no longer serves you. You will simply stop using words like really and much. Thus your sentence becomes 'I'm not a dancer.'"

Martha felt her mind begin to lose its tracking ability. "I dance a little bit."

"That's better," Aurora said. "If I translate that for you, it becomes, 'I dance.'"

Martha seemed startled. She knew then for certain that she would be dancing later. It felt like something she could not resist; already a languid, fluid motion was pulling her.

In the evening Martha pulled on the clothes Aurora had given her, black leggings and a long, buff-colored shirt with black spots. She stood in front of the mirror in her room when she was ready, thinking about her recent dream of turning into a jaguar. "Dance from your heart," Aurora said when she came for her. "Let the dance arise from the essence of who you are. You will feel a power take over and begin to move through you. You will become one with it. It is how the jaguar will emerge."

They returned to the sacred spot of the stone circle, which Olivia had already prepared. Aurora explained that the spirits of the animals had been called in and told her she might see them during her dance. As Aurora lit a fire in the center of the circle, Martha put on her jaguar mask, which had been set out for her. "Begin when you are ready," Aurora said. Then she and Olivia left.

It was dark. The fire cast shadows and crackled as it grew in size. Martha waited, listening, wondering when she should begin and how she would know what to do. Aurora had warned her not to take the mask off once she put it on—the jaguar had been summoned. It would recognize itself in her.

She listened to the sounds of the night. She felt cold and moved closer to the fire. Thinking she heard footsteps, she turned, but in the darkness she saw nothing. An ember popped, showering sparks, then another. As she watched them, mesmerized, the fire began to speak to her with rhythmic crackling and popping sounds, which pulled her to movement. Almost on its own, her body came to life, tracking slowly around the fire, swaying this way and that, in and out of the shadows. Her movements were languid at first and then grew more purposeful. She began stalking. Her senses came to life as she watched and listened and felt the uneven ground beneath her feet. It was a dance of longing and belonging, and it began to pull her back and forth between the human realm and the animal kingdom.

Her human form gave way in the gyrations of her movement. At first she was dancing and then she was being danced. At that moment she entered the place of connection. The jaguar recognized itself in her and merged with her. The dance enveloped her, swirled her as she became one with the motion and one with the stillness inside it. The fire lapped at the darkness as her awareness moved into the shadows. She lost track of how long she danced, it could have been minutes or hours. Her tongue hung from her mouth. Her eyes reflected the flames. Her feet padded on the ground. Presently her movement slowed. There were eyes watching. At the edge of the light cast by the fire she became aware of the animals—the rabbit, the coyote, the deer, the mouse, the mustang, the hawk, the wolf, the bear, the otter, the eagle, the raven. So many had come to join her in the circle. They spoke to her in their voices and she understood them. One by one they entered the dance with her, until they were all moving as one. They had answered her invitation with an invitation of their own, to meet in the realm of inherent knowing. She saw them for the first time as multidimensional beings, indistinguishable from herself. She had crossed into a world of unity, unhindered by fear or judgment or inequality. There was nothing within her capable of causing harm, and nothing within them that could harm her. Everything was as it should be, and she was awestruck by the majestic interrelationship.

It was a moment of transition. Something within her changed. She had touched a reality of undeniable serenity. It was irresistible, and she felt herself give way. The sweetness encompassed her, like the fragrance of spring blossoms. She had discovered a world that until now she thought was imaginary. But here it was, big as life and better even than she could dream. Her spirit was willing and available, and she entered the experience with her whole being.

As she sat by the dying embers, Martha heard a sound. She looked up to discover Aurora. "They have made you an ally," she said, wrapping a shawl around Martha's shoulders. "You can call on them for assistance. I can see you are tired. I will tell you more later." She guided Martha to the portal, and they returned to the school.

Wrapped in the shawl, Martha lay down on her bed and fell into a deep sleep. In her dream, the jaguar came to her. It spoke. "In the dance I gave myself to you. You gave yourself to me. We now move as one. When you are ready, you can walk between the worlds."

When she woke it was still dark and she padded soundlessly out to the pool in her slippers. She was still wearing the clothes she had danced in, and she pulled the shawl around her tightly. Aurora came with tea and nuts and fresh fruit. Martha realized she was famished. She was unusually quiet, and Aurora respected her silence, simply sitting with her.

Finally Aurora spoke. "Things will be different now. The animals will recognize you and will speak to you. Even at home."

Martha nodded.

"They have been waiting for this moment. They await it with all humans. They have missed the connection, lost long ago. They will offer guidance when it's needed, and they will seek guidance when they want it. Sometimes they will simply want to experience the connection."

"I feel that," Martha said.

"Remember when I told you your life would never be the same?"

Martha wondered what was coming next. She had something to tell Aurora, and she was hesitant to do it.

"What is it?" Aurora asked, picking up on her thoughts.

"There's something I need to tell you. I discovered a book that describes the powers of the feather. I was able to read it, although I can't decipher the last one."

"The powers come as you need them, and as you become powerful enough to use them," Aurora said. "Just as Chaco said."

"This would all be a lot…." Realizing she had used a qualifying word, she stopped. "This would all be easier if I could understand him." She stopped. "Wait. I will be able to understand him now." She hesitated before continuing, but she knew she had to speak. "There's something else."

"It's unacceptable what Hocket has done."

"You knew?"

Aurora nodded. "You want to solve this, and you have done an admirable job. Chaco was greatly impressed by your late-night sortie. He had trouble keeping up with you."

"He followed me?"

"He wanted to be sure you were safe. You are a first-rate student."

"I thought he was sleeping."

"Chaco is never asleep," Aurora said. "He is also a master of astral travel. In fact, he prefers that method, especially when it's raining."

"I feel better knowing he has been keeping an eye on things."

"Chaco has a soft place in his heart for you."

"And I have become fond of him," Martha said.

"Remember that he is a master. And as a Level 3, he is aware of all things at all times." She grew reflective. "It is time to call in the Trackers. There is some risk, but I believe they can help."

"The Trackers?" Martha looked at Aurora for elaboration.

"Yes, they will hone in on the feather's location and take you to it."

"What is the risk?"

"They love active duty," she said. "The risk is their aggressiveness, their reluctance to give up the chase once you are done. Don't let them turn on you. It takes a level head and a certain amount of finesse to control them."

"How will I get it, if it's locked up somewhere?"

"You have many techniques available to you. You will know what to do. Remember that you need not work on this plane. You can sometimes be most effective in another dimension. Think about the portal, for instance. If I had an exact answer, I would tell you. I am only a teacher. You will easily surpass me in ability once you embrace your true power. Don't be limited by what I have not been able to tell you."

Martha wasn't sure what surprised her more when she stepped into her garden later that day—the magnificent Mexican fountain that had been installed or the iguana that was sunning itself on an adjacent stone. It was the fountain she had dreamed of having— three ornate tiers with water cascading from the top bowl into a larger middle bowl and finally into the pool at the base, which was at least ten feet across. It looked like it had been there for years. Next to it there were several potted birds of paradise with exotic red flowers.

The iguana had a deep voice and began chatting with her at once. She was surprised to find that he had a sense of humor and was very droll and playful. Just as she asked him why he was there they were interrupted by the sound of someone coming through the gate. "I thought I heard your voice," Ned said, materializing a moment later. She motioned to him to sit down, and he had just begun to settle into a chair when he spotted the iguana. "My God, a dragon!" He nearly toppled over trying to get out of the way.

"Careful," Martha said. "You don't want to startle him."

"Startle *him*? Of course not." Ned struggled to regain his composure, taking a position behind the chair. "What is that? And what is it doing here?"

"It's an iguana," Martha stated. "He's sitting in the sun, like I am. He is actually quite shy, by the way—but very opinionated."

"First one I've seen," Ned replied, feeling safe enough to sit now that he knew the creature would not be breathing fire. "Can't for the life of me imagine what they would have an opinion about."

"Quite a few things, but especially the quality of the sun. It's not what he's used to and he doesn't imagine he'll stay long."

Ned was surprised. "You sound like you were talking to him."

"Yes. He's sorry that he startled you, by the way."

Ned nodded. "Then tell him we're even. The fountain is spectacular," he added. "It was here when we got back from the golf course. Pretty fast work."

"Isn't it lovely? It is exactly the fountain I wanted." She reached over to put her hand in the water.

Ned watched the cascading water while he considered what to say next. Finally he spoke. "A week ago I didn't believe any of this," he said, measuring his words. "But it's hard not to believe what I can see with my own eyes. However, you seem like an unlikely person to have these experiences."

"I totally agree," Martha said. "I resisted it, I must say. But finally I saw that no matter what I did, it was going to happen."

"Does that necklace have something to do with it? I notice you never take it off."

"Yes. It's ancient. It's been handed down along with certain powers."

"Like flying."

She nodded.

"Do I dare ask what else?"

"As far as I can tell, the powers arrive when I'm ready," she replied. "I never know I can do something until I do it." She paused, wondering about her newest ability—walking between the worlds. She wasn't sure what that entailed and was so concerned about recovering the feather that she had forgotten to ask Aurora. In fact, Aurora had been on the verge of telling her something; now she wondered what it was.

Ned interrupted her thoughts. "Are you saying you didn't know the car could fly till we went off the road?" He grew serious, picturing what could have happened.

"Yes. For some reason, it popped into my mind that we could fly. I am happy I thought of it."

The fanfare about the UFO had settled down somewhat, and Carol still had no clue her car had been zipping around like a spaceship. They chuckled about that.

"Wouldn't mind doing that again," he mused.

"There's something I have to do," she said. "Maybe you could help me."

"It would be my pleasure," he said without hesitation, hoping it involved flying.

"Before you agree, perhaps you should hear what it is." With that, she began to detail a plan. "We'll wait for dark," she said. "Meet me in the garden then."

Ned could barely contain his excitement during dinner. Three times his sister asked him what was wrong. "You seem agitated," she said. "What is it?"

"I'm meeting Martha later for a stroll," he said.

"I'm not sure you should keep seeing her," Carol said. "She seems a bit odd. Don't you think, Joe?"

"I haven't noticed anything," Joe said, focusing on his potatoes.

"You haven't noticed anything? I think she's up to something but I don't know what. Yet," she emphasized. "Yes, she is definitely up to something. And I noticed that the only time she invited you over was when I was gone. And now she's after Ned."

"She's not after me," Ned said. "Why do you like to see the worst in people?"

"Oh, now I'm to blame, is that it?" Carol said. "I'm the one who always looked after your best interests as your older sister, and now I'm to blame. That hurts."

Ned knew he couldn't win, so he quit.

"If I can remind you, you're a guest here. The least you can be is appreciative. We invited you here to cheer you up, isn't that right, Joe." Joe stared at his plate. "You seem so down in the mouth since Barb died. And now you're telling me I see the worst in people. Joe, are you going to back me up?"

"I think you should mind your own business," Joe said. "Let Ned have a life."

"You think what?" Carol sputtered. "You are going to regret telling me that." She pushed abruptly away from the table and left the room.

"Do you want the game on?" Joe asked when she was gone. "Or do you want to enjoy the silence?"

"It may be time for me to head home," Ned replied. "I've overstayed my welcome."

"Not at all. Stay as long as you like. To tell you the truth, I really enjoy having you here. I should have said something to Carol before this. She thinks everybody should jump when she says so."

Joe stood up to get them some dessert. "Not for me," Ned said. "I need to be going." He was trying to remember Martha's instructions. Bring a sandwich and a passport. He didn't have a passport, but why would he need one? After all, they weren't leaving the country. There wasn't time for that. Certainly they wouldn't even be leaving Seaport, he thought, sticking a sandwich into his pocket.

14

Following the beam of his flashlight, Ned made his way to a bench in the garden. He kicked at a stone, still upset about Carol. If she could just stop being critical, he thought, she might have an easier time of it. Pointing out another person's flaws temporarily relieved her own painful feelings of inadequacy, but it was like taking aspirin for a broken leg. It didn't fix the problem. But she'd been a fault-finder his whole life, and he wasn't going to change her.

He swung the light around in the darkness, searching for Martha. Perhaps he should have knocked on her door. He expected her to be here by now. It was a windless night with no moon, and the shadows played tricks with his eyes. He leaned forward on the bench, looking in the direction of the house.

A sudden sound made him turn. It came from the overgrown area behind him. He shone the flashlight into the brush, but saw nothing. Then someone called his name, as if from very far away. In the distance he heard a rumble.

"Martha? Is that you?"

What seemed like a breeze tossed the branches, and the rumble began to hum, as if an army of insects was approaching. A moment later, dozens of small creatures that looked like winged mice swarmed around him, buzzing and flying at his face. He swatted wildly, which only made it worse, and they continued to swarm.

"Ned, there you are!" Martha waved a hand at the flying crea-tures. "As one," she commanded and they immediately came togeth-er, hovering soundlessly in a giant group. "Are you all right?"

He was still swatting. "What the—?"

She interrupted. "They're Trackers. They're going to help us. I had to go and summon them."

"Summon them? From where?"

"Their home. It's…I'll tell you later. There's no time now. Come." She set off down a small path and he quickly followed. "Now," she said, turning to face him, "you will have to trust me. We are going to follow the Trackers where they take us. What you need to do is hang on, like that day we were flying over the river."

"Are we going to be flying? It's a little hard to see in the dark. It would help if the moon was out."

"The moon won't be any help where we're going," she an-nounced, causing Ned to shiver. "I would have taken Angela, but she's dog-sitting for her sister's terriers. So it's up to you. Just listen carefully to my instructions. Hold on."

The next thing Ned knew, he was weightless and unable to move, as if he was suspended in time and space. Yet he was moving, or being moved. The feeling was so strange that he closed his eyes, but as soon as he did he felt himself land. When he opened his eyes, nothing was familiar. "Where are we?" he managed to croak.

Martha held a finger to her lips to silence him. She was staring at something, or through something, but he couldn't tell what.

"I think we're in the right place," she said in a low voice. "It's important to move carefully, and watch your step. You don't want to break through."

"Break through what?" He surveyed his surroundings for a clue, but everything was out of focus. "I must need glasses," he whis-pered. "Everything's fuzzy."

"We are in an adjacent dimension. At least I hope so. I'll know in a minute."

Ned squinted to see if that helped him see more clearly. "This can't be."

Martha stopped and turned, her expression dead serious. "Ned, I can't have you being negative. You must imagine that this is possible, no matter what. You have to give up your ideas of what you think is possible if you are going to help me. But tell me now. Because if you can't do this, I will take you back and go on alone."

Ned looked away, embarrassed. "No, no, I want to help," he said. "Just tell me what to do." He suddenly felt more like Carol than he wanted to admit. In some ways, he thought, he was behaving like her right now. Martha was asking him to see things from a different perspective, and he couldn't do it.

"Ned, stay with me." She had moved off while he was daydreaming, and he hurried to catch up. His eyes were beginning to adjust. "Is that Seaport?" he asked.

"Yes." She was focused on what she was doing, and talking seemed to distract her, so he followed quietly as they moved along a street. The moon had come up, and the light made everything glow. He said hello to someone they passed, but the man didn't respond. "Good, he couldn't see you," Martha said as a dog ran out from a yard, barking at them. "The dog can. Keep moving."

"There's Carol," he said as a familiar car drove by. "She's upset with me."

"Pay attention. We have to stay with the Trackers, so watch where they go. They're moving fast."

He had just noticed they were darting in and out as they buzzed along, as if they were searching every nook and cranny. Martha stayed right with them, seeming to float. Ned was becoming used to the texture of the air as if brushed against his face. He checked his watch. It had stopped. He was having trouble keeping up, and he called to her.

"You're not staying focused," she said, not turning. "You need to focus on following or you'll get lost."

A jolt of alarm went through his body, and he realized he had to keep up. Adrenaline surged, and his movements became faster and more coordinated.

The Trackers had grown increasingly animated, and their pace increased. Martha stepped up her pace as well. Ned was beginning to breathe hard, and he wondered how Martha was managing this. She barely seemed to touch the ground. He, on the other hand, seemed to be walking through mud. The harder he tried, the more his body resisted. He forced himself to focus. Just when he thought he was going to collapse, it happened. He began to float. It became easy. The more he relaxed, the less effort he needed. He began to enjoy the view, watching people without being seen. He kept one eye on Martha.

Suddenly the Trackers were swirling in a frenzy of activity. "They've found something," she said, getting closer but not so close that they were banging into her. She peered through what looked like a watery wall. They were outside of a house. "They're going in," she said, and off the Trackers swooped in a mass of buzzing.

Ned shut his eyes as they swept through a window and into a living room. Henry Hocket was reading in a recliner. Martha motioned to Ned to be silent, but the professor looked around as if something was amiss. Ned held his breath, motionless. He couldn't be seen, but could he be heard? Or sensed?

The Trackers nosed around the living room like bloodhounds in a fury of exploration. The professor had gone back to reading, but now he put his book down and frowned. At the same moment the Trackers swept down the hall and through a door that was closed. Ned was sucked in behind them.

In the study, Ned felt it was safe to breathe again. "Can he hear us?" he whispered, pointing.

Martha shrugged, watching the Trackers with great interest as they hovered around a cabinet. "It's in there, I know it," she said. She reached out to open it but was unable to touch it. "Here's where I need help." Her voice was urgent. "Block the door to the room. I'm going to step across for a moment."

"Wait. Don't leave me," Ned said. "I have no idea how to go back."

"I'll just be a moment." He watched her step through into the room. She approached the cabinet and opened it. There were books and papers inside and she began to look through them. The Trackers were agitated. They zoomed this way and that and occasionally attacked the cabinet. Ned positioned himself in front of the door as she tried the drawers. As she reached for the last one, the door to the room flew open and Ned lost his balance. Hocket walked in. Flabbergasted, he stared at Martha. When he regained his composure, his voice was like ice.

"I knew it was you the night of the storm." His eyes blazed.

"You've taken something that isn't rightfully yours," she said. "I want it back."

"Why would it be given to someone like you?"

His words stung, and her anger flared. "As opposed to someone like you?" The question was out of her mouth before she could stop it.

Hocket reached into his desk and pulled out a gun. "I would hate to have to use this, but you can understand my predicament. Someone has broken into my house, a burglar, it seems."

Martha felt her heart in her throat but she spoke calmly. "Don't be rash."

He raised the gun, pointing it directly at her.

Ned watched as if electrified, wondering what he could do. The Trackers were moving like missiles and he felt them whiz by his head.

"I'm not alone," she said.

Henry's head swiveled. "What do you mean?"

"There's someone watching your every move, so let's be sensible. I know the feather is here. The Trackers brought me here, and they are never wrong."

He looked confused. "Who's with you?"

"I am," Ned said. He waved his arms to no avail. "Look."

"I thought so. You're alone. Let's go."

But Ned was not to be deterred. "I am here," he said so force-fully that his disembodied voice reverberated in the room.

Alarmed, Henry gripped the gun. "Who's there?"

"I have come for my feather." Ned's voice rumbled in the small room.

Henry grew pale. His hand began to tremble. "I want it for re-search. I mean no harm. Who is it?" he asked Martha.

"You must return it at once," Ned boomed. "Before harm is done. Your gun is useless." Henry let his arm drop to his side. Martha thought about jumping for the weapon, like she had seen in movies. "Now!" Ned's voice rattled the windows.

"I can explain everything," Henry said, still looking around, vainly trying to see who was there. But all at once he looked at Martha. "There's no one here," he said. "It's only a voice. I am not giving you the feather. It's mine now."

No sooner did he speak than a tremendous noise filled the small room. It was so loud that Martha covered her ears. The Trackers had burst through from the adjacent dimension, and they swarmed Henry, ferociously nipping and biting. He shouted for them to stop. Martha quickly opened the last drawer and saw the feather. "We did it," she said.

Henry was swatting like mad to protect himself.

She called the Trackers, and with a whoosh she was out of the room, back behind the watery layer. The Trackers swarmed around the feather. "We've found it. Now home," she said.

But where was Ned? She wanted to thank him for his brilliant assistance, but he was nowhere to be seen. She took one last glance back at Henry, wildly turning as if he didn't understand what had happened. When he saw the open drawer was empty, his face grew dark.

But she had something more important to worry about. She turned to the Trackers. "Find Ned," she said.

For the next two hours, they searched, until Martha was exhausted. It was well past midnight. Where had he gone? She was overcome with fear. How could she explain this to Carol and Joe? If she did tell them, they would want to call the police, and she knew the authorities would be of no help. Of course, she could wait until morning, and resume her search by the light of day. But something told her time was of the essence.

Returning home, she called Ned's name in the garden just in case, and then, after putting the feather in a safe place, she went to check the McIntyre's house. It was dark, save for a light in the kitchen. Hoping that maybe he'd gone there, she stole across the moonlit yard. She had decided not to ring the bell so as not to alarm them. That meant she had to look in the window like a peeping tom. She pushed through the forsythia bushes and stood beside the window for a minute working up the nerve to actually look in. When she saw Carol eating a bowl of cereal at the table, looking glum, Martha almost rapped on the glass. But it didn't feel right.

Instead she made her way around to the side where the guest-room was. The ladder was up against the house, put there to wash the windows on the second floor. As quietly as possible, she stepped onto it and began to climb. She'd never done anything remotely this brazen, and her heart was racing. But she had to know if Ned was home.

But he wasn't in his room. She started back down when she heard a sound. Just below she saw Joe in his pajamas, rolling up the hose. Carol, unable to sleep, must have sent him out. Martha panicked as she realized he was going to put away the ladder. What could she tell him about what she was doing, when it looked like she was climbing out of Ned's window?

She would have to fly. As he walked toward the ladder she leapt into the air and landed on the other side of the hedge. "Who's there?" Joe asked. She ducked into the bushes and made her way quickly to her door. She watched Joe haul the ladder into the garage and then stepped into the portal. She hoped Aurora was awake.

The courtyard of the school was deserted, and she walked quietly to Aurora's room. She was tired, and she wanted nothing more than to sleep. She stared longingly at the comfortable chairs by the pool, wanting to cover up with a thick towel and succumb to their softness. The fragrance of gardenia blossoms enveloped her, carried on the night air, and she was momentarily revived.

After listening for a moment outside the door, she knocked.

As it turned out, Aurora was up. A fire was lit in the fireplace, and several candles illuminated the room. In spite of the hour, the teacher was expecting her. As the story spilled out, Aurora listened carefully. When she answered, she was too serious. "You're right to be concerned. I am uncertain why you took him with you, as he has no experience."

Martha tried to explain. "I needed someone to help. Without him...well, I don't know what would have happened."

"At some time, you have to trust yourself and your abilities," Aurora said quietly.

"I thought we were supposed to work together. I thought that was the whole idea."

"Yes, that is important. First comes trusting yourself. Once you trust yourself, anything is possible. Until that moment, you are jeopardizing everyone. If you can't be there for yourself, you can't be there for anyone else."

Martha felt too tired to have this conversation. "I just need to find him," she said. "I don't know what to do. I can't leave him stranded. Where do you think he is?"

"Chaco will look for him. Now go home and we will talk again soon. For the time being, say nothing."

Martha didn't argue. Instead, she walked out into the courtyard and stood there under the stars. She hoped Ned was OK. Perhaps Aurora was right, that she shouldn't have taken him. But really, what would she have done against Hocket alone? She was so exhausted she could no longer think clearly. She stepped into the portal. She wanted nothing more than to crawl into bed and go to sleep. In a few moments, she would be home. But as she thought about home, she felt a rush of cold air that seemed unfamiliar and unwelcome. She began to fall, spiraling out of control. Desperately she fought to get back to the courtyard, but instead she fell.

15

Like a boulder bouncing down a cliff, Martha tumbled for several minutes. When she finally managed to get control, the landscape was dark and unfamiliar. Not far away, she spotted a wrought iron fence, and as she wondered if she was inside of it, a large dog rushed up and began barking furiously at her. With relief she saw it was on the other side.

Lights appeared in the house, and the dog grew increasingly agitated. Two men, speaking Spanish, called to the dog, sweeping their powerful flashlights over the grounds. Martha headed into the shadows and ducked behind a tree. She held her breath as the lights played around her. Finally she heard the men moving away, their voices growing fainter.

She could see lights to the east—a city. There was a road not far from her and she started walking, reluctant to use the portal again. When the headlights of a car lit up the road, she stepped off to the side, not wanting to be seen. She tried to read the license plate, hoping it would tell her where she was.

A second car approached and again she moved off the road into the brush. After it went by she resumed walking. But the car U-turned and headed back, catching her directly in its headlights.

"Need a lift?" A woman's head poked out of an open window on the driver's side.

"Sheila?"

"I thought that was you." Sheila gave Martha a bright smile. "What are you doing here? It must be a portal mishap."

"Where am I?"

"Tucson, Arizona. I live just up the road. I was over at a friend's house for dinner. So how'd you get here?"

Martha began to explain as she got in the car. She was so relieved the words came out in a rush.

"Slow down," Sheila said. "I'm having trouble following this. Who's Ned?"

Martha relayed the details as Sheila drove. As they pulled into her driveway, Martha said she couldn't stay. "I'll be a nervous wreck until we find Ned."

"Are you sure you don't want to get some sleep and head home first thing in the morning?" At the mention of sleep, Martha remembered how late it was. She very much wanted to sleep, but if Ned got back, no one would know where she was.

"I'll send a Teller to Aurora. They love to be the first to spill the news about anything. They're nothing but gossips really, but very useful ones in situations like these."

"I haven't used them," Martha admitted, following Sheila into her spacious adobe house. She admired the warm and inviting interior as Sheila flicked on some lights. "I love the way you've decorated."

"I'm passionate about color," Sheila said, setting her purse on the kitchen counter. "I enjoy simplicity and clean, smooth lines. Care for a glass of water, or something stronger?"

"Water, thank you." Martha ran her hand over a large, smooth sculpture in the living room. "This is beautiful. Who's the artist?"

"It's one of mine. That's my other career, when I'm not gallivanting around taking classes in metaphysics."

"I had no idea. I'm impressed."

"Thank you," Sheila said. "I love sculpting, allowing a form to emerge. It's very satisfying. I especially love creating women. When I was in Boston I saw a Degas, one of his life-size dancers. I was struck by the way that he had captured movement in stillness. The piece had so much life that I expected the ballerina to begin dancing at any moment. That's what I want to incorporate in my work."

"Speaking of dancing, I wish I had a picture of my dance the other night. I would commission you to make a sculpture for me."

"Tell me about it."

"It was the Dance of the Jaguar," Martha said. "I don't think of myself as a dancer, so I was taken aback when Aurora told me what I would be doing." There was awe in her voice as she began to relive the experience, which drew Sheila in. "It was a sacred dance, a dance of transformation and power."

"Go on."

Martha stood up. "It was night. There was a blazing fire. Aurora gave me a jaguar mask to wear. Just the act of putting it on began the transformation." Martha felt like she was there again by the fire. "There was no one else around, and as I began to dance, a powerful force took over. I began to move with languid steps, exactly like a cat. I was a cat." She moved across the kitchen like a jaguar, then stopped and looked directly at Sheila. "Had you been there, you would have believed you were watching a jaguar circle the fire. And then something happened that still astounds me."

Sheila took her camera from the counter. Still listening intently, she took several photos.

"The animals came out of the shadows to join me in the dance, every kind of animal, as if we were all one being. At that point, it became more than a dance. It became…a melding of spirits."

Mesmerized by the performance, Sheila suddenly exclaimed, "The dance of transformation! That means you can walk between the worlds."

Martha was surprised. "Yes, that's what the jaguar said."

"I've read about that," Sheila continued, growing animated.

Martha brightened. "Tell me, because I'm not sure what it means."

"That's one reason we go to the Ancient Wisdom School, one of the reasons anyway." Sheila stopped and looked at Martha. "To learn how to do that. Not everyone becomes that powerful. Have you tried it yet?"

Martha frowned. "I don't know what I am supposed to try," she finally admitted.

"All I know is what I've read. Basically, walking between the worlds allows you to move in nonlinear ways. You are no longer limited by time. You are also not limited by space. You can move the way light moves. You can move the way thought moves. You can travel between dimensions. The only limits you have are the limits of your imagination."

"I will need a little more practice," Martha said. "I was trying to go home, and I ended up here." She was too tired to think.

"Your intention has to become like a laser," Sheila said. "You have to be very focused. If you aren't clear you're going to trip yourself."

"That's what must have happened," Martha said. "It was odd, though, because suddenly it was terribly cold. I've never felt that before."

Sheila's face went so pale that Martha grew worried. "What is it?"

"Something I read," she said, looking away.

Martha frowned again. "You must tell me."

"I read that when you feel cold, it is your own doubt. It is dangerous to be in a portal when you feel doubt. I think you should tell Aurora what happened."

Martha was reluctant. "I think I've troubled her enough lately."

"Promise me," Sheila said.

Martha finally agreed. "After I find Ned. He has to be a priority. I still don't know how I lost him."

"Don't wait," Sheila cautioned, turning on the outside lights. "Let's go out on the patio."

As they made their way out, Martha admired a sculpture on the patio. "You're very gifted," she said. "Obviously you sell these."

"My gallery is good to me," Sheila said. "They sell enough to support my two vices—shoes and Harley-Davidsons."

"You ride a motorcycle?" Martha asked in disbelief.

"Stick around long enough tomorrow and I'll take you for a ride."

"My father rode ever so long ago. I haven't been on one since I was a teenager."

"That settles it. Now let's find us a Teller."

Sheila turned on the walkway lights in the back and they wandered into the yard. "The best way to attract one is to gossip about someone. They show up immediately. Oh, to be the first in the know! It makes their little hearts go pitter-patter. But wait, before you do, it has to be the thing you want them to tell. And be sure to tell them *not* to tell the one person you want to know about it. That way they will."

Martha looked around but saw nothing. She began to talk about how she didn't want Aurora to know what had happened. All at once she heard a rustling sound. Sheila nodded. "Message received. Over and out."

Martha wanted to see one. "They're hard to spot," Sheila said. "They're very sneaky. They prefer to work without being seen. That way no one can pin the gossip on them."

Martha was disappointed, so Sheila reassured her. "You'll see one eventually. They do get careless."

Sheila showed Martha the guestroom, and the moment her head hit the pillow, she was asleep. She slept so soundly she didn't hear Sheila stir in the morning, and when Sheila knocked on her door, she dragged herself out of bed. They had breakfast on the patio.

"I feel so much better," Martha said. "Refreshed and renewed."

"Good. Sleep is important. It's very restorative. I read somewhere that we do our most important work when we sleep. We're mending lots of things we messed up when we were awake."

"I wouldn't be surprised. That's probably why our dreams are so wild. What time is it, by the way?"

"Ten."

Martha almost fell out of her chair. "I must get back. What will Carol think if Ned's still missing?"

At that moment they heard a rustling sound. When Martha turned, she saw a small winged creature with beady eyes and big ears. "What on earth?"

"Just listen," Sheila said.

"Carol thinks Ned spent the night with you," the Teller announced with great satisfaction. Since it was all of two inches tall, Martha almost laughed; however, she was too surprised by the message. "She thinks he's rushing into things. Joe told her to mind her own business. She said she thinks you are a—"

Sheila clapped her hands together once. Startled, the Teller nearly toppled over. "Sometimes you have to stop them," she said. "They tend to go on and on."

"I would like to hear some news of Ned," Martha said.

But the Teller disappeared as quickly as it had come. "At least you got to see one," Sheila said.

"I'm not sure I find them useful," Martha noted. "How is news of that sort helpful?"

"You have to read between the lines. You know that Ned's not back, and you know they're not worried yet about that. That gives you some time. Let's take a ride."

Martha had forgotten about the motorcycle. She wasn't in the mood for a ride on the back of one at the moment, but Sheila said she would drive her to a nearby portal. "It's an easy one to use, you can't miss. You'll be home in no time." She handed Martha a helmet and got the bike out of the garage. "Climb aboard and we're off," she said. As they pulled out into the street, Martha felt a thrill. Not having ridden in a long time, she held on tightly. "I forgot how loud they are," she shouted.

"Yes, well, if someone doesn't see us, maybe they'll hear us," Sheila shouted back.

Martha would have enjoyed a longer ride, but there wasn't time. Sheila let her off at a park and pointed. "Right over there, next to the pond, by the bench. I like to wait till no one's around."

"Thank you. I will see you soon," Martha said, swinging her leg over the back of the motorcycle as gracefully as she could.

Sheila put the bike into gear. "Gossip about me when you get home," she said. "That way I'll know you're back."

"Will do," Martha said, waving. She made her way to the bench just as a man with a newspaper appeared and sat down.

"I don't mind sharing," he said. "Feel free to take the other end."

"Oh, I can't stay," Martha said. "I'll just stand here and admire the pond for a moment."

"I haven't seen you here before," he said. "I would know, this is my usual spot."

"I haven't been here before."

He laid his newspaper on his lap and continued to talk, obviously happy to have someone to listen. He sounded like he was just getting warmed up. "If you don't mind," she said, interrupting, "I believe I'll meditate a bit."

"Will it bother you if I talk?" he asked.

"Yes." She moved a few feet behind the bench and closed her eyes. He turned to watch. When she opened her eyes to see if he was reading his paper yet, he was staring right at her.

"Are you done?"

"No, I'm just getting started. It will be awhile," she said, suggesting he read his paper.

"Don't you have to sit down to do that?"

She shook her head. "Standing meditation."

He watched her for a moment. "Actually, I've never seen anyone meditate," he said. "I don't understand the appeal. What do you do, just not think? Or think about nothing? Those are two different things, you know." He chuckled, obviously pleased with himself.

"No talking," she said. "And no staring."

"It's a big park," he said. "You can always find another spot. I told you this is my usual spot. If there's anyone here, I like to talk."

Martha was growing exasperated. All she wanted to do was go home. "What if I teach you to meditate?" It was an impulsive idea that seemed to come out of nowhere, and she suggested it before she could stop herself.

He frowned as he considered the offer. "No thanks," he finally said. "I'll read my paper."

"It's very good for you," she said. "It has all kinds of health benefits. And it's very relaxing. It also—"

"No thanks," he said, more firmly this time. He began to study the front page headlines, giving Martha the opportunity she needed. Quick as a flash, she stepped into the portal. She hoped she didn't have any problems, because she really wanted to go straight home.

When the man turned again to check on her a few minutes later, she was gone. He looked all around, but there was no sign of her. "Humph," he said to himself. "She didn't even say goodbye." He felt some cold air swirl around him, which was unusual for the warm morning, and it unsettled him, as if there was something about it that wasn't good.

It took Martha every ounce of energy she had to get through the frigid air, which chilled her to the bone. She was immensely relieved to get home, and she knew she needed to ask Aurora about the problem as soon as she could. It was making portal travel difficult. But as soon as she arrived at her house, she heard Carol at the door. "There you are! I've been ringing your doorbell. Are you holding Ned hostage?"

"Hasn't he come home yet?"

"Do you think I'd be looking for him if he had?"

"I don't know where he is. Did you have a fight?"

Carol started to cry. "Is that why he didn't come back? Because of that?"

Martha felt like she had opened a can of worms. "I'm sure we'll hear from him."

"What did he tell you?"

"Nothing, actually. He mentioned you were upset, that's all."

"I'm sure he told you more than that."

Martha shook her head, wishing Carol would leave. A moment later Joe poked his head out the door to tell her she had a phone call.

Martha went back in her house, hoping she would have word of Ned soon. She wondered if Chaco had been able to find him. She straightened the living room and cleaned up the kitchen. When he wasn't back by noon, she decided it was time to go look for him. She would go to the last place she had seen him—Hocket's house.

Stepping into her portal, she moved through the area she had traveled earlier with Ned. She searched around Henry's house, but there was no sign of him. The sound of voices drew her attention and she tried to see who it was.

"She'll be back." There was a malicious laugh. "I know she'll come looking for him." It was Henry. He had Ned! But where? She retraced her steps carefully, listening attentively. Finally she found Henry in his office, alone, looking in his desk drawer for something. She screwed up her courage to confront him, hoping she wouldn't lose her nerve. What if she did? Her heart began to pound.

She stepped through the veil separating them, but as she did, the cold air surrounded her. She fought it, but it slowly overcame her, and she felt her energy draining. How was this happening? The last thing she heard as she lost consciousness was Henry. "I knew you'd come," he announced.

16

Sheila waited impatiently by the pool for Aurora. Steven had gone to look for her. Minutes passed, and there was no time to waste. Finally, after what seemed like ages, Aurora arrived. "Steven said it's urgent."

"It's about Martha. I think she's in trouble. Have you heard from her?" When Aurora shook her head, Sheila explained that Martha had come to see her quite by accident. "She was looking for someone named Ned, and she ended up in Tucson. She said she had felt very cold air in the portal. I just know she was feeling the cloud of doubt. I told her it was dangerous."

Aurora raised her eyebrows.

"I know we haven't learned about that yet in class," Sheila continued quickly, "but I've been reading on my own." As if to give ominous emphasis to her words, a single cloud enveloped the sun at that moment. "If she doubts her power…."

Aurora quickly scanned the sky. "It is hard to keep up with all of you," she said. "It happens with some classes, everyone goes in different directions instead of focusing on what we're teaching. This group is the most challenging ever. Steven says it's because you are all so diversely talented." Aurora frowned. "She made it through?"

"Yes, and I asked her to talk to you about it. She didn't want to bother you. Finally she said she would, after she found her friend who is missing."

"Ah, yes. Chaco is looking for him."

"I'm afraid Martha has gone on her own."

"Why do you think so?" Aurora's alarm was disconcerting to Sheila.

"She's not home," Sheila confided. "A little bit ago I began to feel uneasy, so I went to check on her. She's not there. Her neighbors haven't seen her since this morning."

"I see." Aurora was silent, contemplating this information. Finally she spoke. "I need to talk with Steven and Olivia. What you are suggesting is very serious. I am not certain what we can do. Our mission here is to teach you, to give you the skills you need. Beyond that, we cannot be much help. Martha is very powerful, and she doesn't fully understand her power yet. This is always the most challenging time for students, when they are learning what they can do. Occasionally, they get into difficult situations." As Aurora left to find the other teachers, she thanked Sheila for coming. "We'll do what we can," she said.

Sheila felt worried. She had hoped Aurora would have an easy answer to ensure her friend's safety. Instead, she now suspected Martha was in grave danger. She wished she could help, but she had barely begun to use her portal skills. As a beginner, what could she do? There was only one thing she could think of, and time was of the essence.

Martha slowly became aware of being cold. She shivered, wishing she had a jacket or a blanket. The light was dim, making it hard to see where she was. Her brain felt foggy, and she struggled to remember something Aurora told her. Even though it was important, it escaped her at the moment, and she refocused on her surroundings. She was on the ground. No wonder she was cold! She moved her foot and it brushed against something. Pulling it quickly back, she sat quietly for a few seconds, then reached out again to see what it was. It was fabric, and as she touched it with her hand she realized it was clothing. Someone else was there with her!

She moved closer to see who it was. She was so surprised—and then relieved—to discover it was Ned that it took her a minute to realize he wasn't moving. An enormous fear gripped her as she recognized that she was in serious danger. She was somewhere the Trackers had been unable—or unwilling—to go, and she had no idea how she had gotten here. She also had no idea how to get out.

She stood up and began to explore. It seemed like she was in a cave, and she moved around looking for an exit. When she heard voices, she hurried back to where she had been and closed her eyes, pretending to be in the same state Ned was.

The voices grew closer until they were at hand. A light filled the space she was in. She lay very still. "They're still out," a man said. "It shouldn't be much longer." When she was sure they were gone, she set to work. Whatever she did, it had to be fast. There wasn't much time. She had to rouse Ned; she wasn't leaving without him. She shook him several times, but he didn't respond. She felt close to panic, and she knew she had to calm herself.

Her heart was pounding. She couldn't focus. All she could think about was the danger she faced. Why couldn't she think of a solution?

Suddenly she did remember what Aurora had said, to trust herself. If she wasn't there for herself, she couldn't be there for anyone. She had to put herself first, no matter what, even though it went against what she had been taught growing up, to always think of others. Although it was uncomfortable to think in this new way, it was all she had right now. She had to save herself.

Leaving Ned's side, she quickly scouted the large cavern once more, feeling her way in the dim light. This time she discovered the passageway the two men had come through. It appeared to be the only way out. Would she encounter them if she used it? Her legs were shaking so much she could barely walk.

All at once, she remembered the amulet around her neck. She reached up to touch it. Unbelievably, it was still there. Hocket hadn't taken that, at least. She had never called upon its power and wasn't sure how to, but if there was ever a time, it was now. Just then, she heard Ned moan and sit up, and she hurried over to him. "You're awake!"

"What? Martha? Is that you?" He sounded both incredulous and relieved.

"Shh. I don't want them to hear us."

"What happened? Where are we?"

"I don't know. Do you have any idea?" She hoped he could shed some light on the situation. Perhaps he had overheard a conversation, something that could help her with what to do now.

"The last thing I remember I was trying to help you." He groaned and rubbed his head.

"Don't talk," she said. "Save your strength. You're going to need it."

Suddenly she heard a rustling sound. She prayed that it wasn't a bat. Then something landed on her shoulder. She tried to scream, but nothing came out. Ned had quickly clapped a hand over her mouth.

They heard a small voice. "Sheila said if you were smarter you would know what to do."

"Who's that?" Ned asked, surprised. He pulled out his pocket flashlight and turned it on. The beam illuminated a Teller, which immediately flitted out of the light. Ned pointed the flashlight around, trying to find the small creature. "What does it mean, smarter? Who's Sheila?"

"Just listen. We have to read between the lines," Martha whispered. She turned to the Teller. "I think I'm quite smart," she said.

"Not smart enough. You went through the cold cloud. You've forgotten the way back. That's what happens. And you don't even know that." Its little voice sounded quite serious.

"I see," Martha said. "I'm not sure why I would need to know that."

"Sheila's right. If you were smarter you would back up time so you could remember."

"Sheila is such a know-it-all," Martha said to Ned. "If we weren't stuck in a cave, I would tell her myself."

"I'll tell her," the Teller said. And with that it flew off.

"Now you've done it," Ned said.

"I had to let her know I found you. And where we are," Martha said. Ned looked confused. "I'll explain later. There isn't time now," she added. "I have to back up to where I remember. You listen to hear if anyone is coming while I do this," she instructed Ned.

Ned did as he was told, not fully comprehending but realizing the dire predicament they were in. Meanwhile, Martha grew quiet. She kept one hand on the amulet. Ned switched off the flashlight to preserve the batteries. After a bit he heard something. "They're coming!" he said, startling Martha. "Quick, what do we do?"

But there wasn't time to do anything before Hocket and his companion arrived, carrying a lantern. "Ah, look what we have here. What a quaint scene. I bet you are wishing you had left well enough alone, aren't you, Martha?"

Martha said nothing. In the light from the lantern she studied the other man, but she didn't recognize him.

"I'm willing to deal," he said. "I will let your friend go in exchange."

"I'm not leaving her," Ned said. "Either we both go, or we both stay."

"Always a gentleman," Hocket replied. "How touching. In this case, you're not being very smart."

"We already know that," Ned said. "Somebody already told us."

"Who?"

Martha looked at Ned to silence him.

"Who was here?" Hocket said, growing edgy and pulling out his gun. He backed up to the passageway he had come through, in case he needed to make a fast exit. His companion remained silent, watching everything like a hawk.

Martha suddenly knew what she had to do. A feeling of power surged through her as she thought about it, surprising her. Her uneasiness vanished. Unless she stood up to Henry, he would win. She had been entrusted with the amulet for a reason. Even if she didn't understand it, she needed to believe it. She needed to release her fear and her feelings of inadequacy. She needed to stop blocking the power that was rising within her. With a dawning realization she saw that her power, which she had never completely experienced, was the source of who she was. "That's it," she said under her breath.

"What was that?" Hocket asked. His jumpiness concerned her. She was afraid he might accidentally pull the trigger. Even if his shot missed, the bullet would ricochet around the cavern. They'd all be endangered.

"You have lied about everything," Martha said. "You have misrepresented what you were up to." Hocket's anger flared as she continued. "What you have done has been about you, not about science or helping anyone else. It was only about your personal desire for power and control."

"It's useless," he said. "You're only a woman. Women believe they have no power. They have always done what they're told, they've never challenged the status quo successfully. Who do you think you are to challenge me?"

"It's not who I think I am," Martha said, growing more confident with every passing second, "it's who I know I am. You might want to believe I am powerless because I am a woman, but that is not the case. You are fooling yourself if you believe I am powerless."

"No," Hocket screamed. "You have no power. It's all lies. The power is mine! I can prove it. If I have the feather, everything is mine. Tell them." He gestured at his companion, who stood mute.

"If you have the feather, it's all yours," the man repeated. "Or so you say."

"Stop it," Hocket said to him. "I've taught you everything you know and given you everything you have. Your only job is to stand behind me one hundred percent. So keep quiet and do what I say."

"Henry," Martha continued. "Power is not seized, it's owned. And as people own their power, it is no longer yours to misuse. You have been using power that isn't yours. That is very clear to me now. The only power you can truthfully use is your own. But that would require you to be honest about what you are doing. You aren't willing to do that. You are like a leech, sucking the power from others to feed your own greed. That is a cowardly way to live."

Hocket was enraged. His fury erupted and he began screaming at everyone, swinging the gun wildly. His companion ducked and tried to grab his arm. Henry broke free. Martha grabbed Ned by the arm and a moment later they were gone. The cold was intense, and she felt buffeted by intense forces, but she focused on her goal, her house. Her intention was unwavering. They landed in a heap, exhausted and out of breath, and the first thing Martha saw was a pair of yellow eyes staring at her.

As it turned out, they belonged to Chaco. She didn't even realize where they were until Ned announced, "We're home!"

She suggested that he let Carol know he was OK. She was eager to sit down and do absolutely nothing for a few minutes. But one look in the kitchen and she knew that was impossible. The drawers were hanging open, every cupboard had been ransacked. She made her way into the family room. The bookshelf was emptied. Her heart sank. Her moment of triumph was over as quickly as it had begun. Henry had come to search for the book. She went immediately to her knitting bag and looked inside. Unbelievably it was still there. So was the feather. But with a sense of foreboding, she realized there was no telling what he would do.

Sinking into her chair, she felt her triumph of the last few minutes drain out of her. She thought she had stepped into her power and done what she needed to do, and now it seemed that it wasn't done at all. Things were worse than they had ever been. Perhaps she didn't understand what this was about. A man like Henry, who had seemed like simply an eccentric professor, would apparently stop at nothing. So what if she could fly or travel through portals or unlock her hidden knowledge. Perhaps she wasn't up to the challenge. It didn't make sense to her. Why was she being asked to do these things? This was more than risky, it was crazy. Maybe what Henry said about her was true. Maybe she was just dreaming if she thought she could be the person she felt like inside.

She needed to go see Aurora. More than likely she had gotten the amulet by mistake. Surely there was someone younger and more vital—and far more powerful—who deserved it more than she, and who could give Henry the fight that would be required.

17

Martha was enjoying a slice of papaya by the pool. Aurora had summoned her unexpectedly without saying why, but she didn't mind sitting here in the early morning to wait. She felt a sense of anticipation, not only to learn why she had been called, but also because dawn promised a new day. She had brought the book about the quetzal to give it to the school, where it would be safe. She was also ready to tell Aurora about her decision.

Above the wall of the school, fingers of sunlight poked through the palm trees, permeating the darkness and chasing off the chill. Martha thought about everything that had happened to her recently. Her life had changed dramatically in recent weeks, but she was prepared to give that up. She poured her first cup of tea and admired the bougainvillea that adorned the wall with showy pink and deep red flowers. It seemed to bloom with all its being, and for a while, she simply stared at it. That's what she felt like lately, she thought, like she was in bloom. She had looked forward to every day and even the unpredictable new experiences that had come her way, because she was blooming. She was finally finding out who she was and expressing her essence like the bougainvillea was, in a profusion of color. Even though she looked the same, she felt very different, because a sense of joy had begun to infuse her daily activities.

That is, until yesterday. Yesterday, for the first time, she sensed she was in over her head. She had begun to lose her confidence. She didn't understand what Henry was up to, and why he had shown up.

She had left her house a few moments ago when it was still dark. And now the sun was peeking brightly over the wall: like the iguana had said, the light was different here; it seemed more intense.

"Ah, first light." It was Aurora. She wandered over and sat down on an adjacent chaise. "This is my favorite time, even more than sunset. It is when the darkness is submissive, when it bows down to the light, when the shadows are chased out into the open. Although you will notice, the shadows never leave. They simply move around. Shadows are very clever that way."

"You make them sound alive," Martha said. She poured a cup of steaming tea and handed it to Aurora, then poured more for herself.

"Everything is alive," Aurora responded. "Even the shadows."

"I have never thought about them like that."

"They are especially lively around a fire," Aurora continued. "They dance in the presence of fire, in the same way that trees dance in the presence of wind, and water dances around rocks."

"The world I have lived in is so different from this."

"It is the same world. All that has changed is the way you see it. When we allow ourselves to be fully alive, then everything around us becomes that way too. At that point our relationship with the world changes. We begin to notice everything. We begin to be aware of the intercommunication." She took a sip of her tea and looked off in the distance. "You are in the process of becoming a powerful woman. You have never seen, felt, or experienced this. Allow yourself to do this."

Martha thought about her words and then asked what she meant by intercommunication.

"We're communicating with everything, and everything is communicating with us—the rocks, the rivers, the oceans, the trees. The spirit world is speaking to us all the time. It is up to us to listen."

Martha felt much like she had that first day in the hut. She began to listen from a deep place inside that seemed to understand. When she was with Aurora, she always had more clarity. Aurora had explained it by saying that Martha was experiencing Aurora's expanded consciousness. She had told her that soon it would be natural for her to feel that way even when she wasn't in Aurora's presence.

"Our conditioning teaches us how to see the world. We are conditioned to behave in a certain way, and that conditioning causes us to act—how do you say it—as if we are on autopilot. We don't think. We aren't even aware of why we are doing something. Often we are frustrated by our behavior, but we cannot see why we act in a certain way."

Martha thought about that, remembering some of her interactions with Murray. She had let him make decisions. He liked making them, and it saved her having to do it. Even now, she found it difficult to make decisions for herself, although she liked how she felt when she did. But she realized she had been conditioned, growing up, to leave decision making to others.

"That's a good example," Aurora said, picking up on her thoughts. "You were giving away your power to make decisions, because you were taught to do that. You were therefore uncomfortable to make your own decisions, were you not?" Martha nodded. It was still somewhat disconcerting to realize Aurora could hear her thoughts, but it didn't startle her as much. "It is simply a matter of relearning," Aurora continued. "And of recognizing that you may feel uncomfortable for a time with doing things in a new way. After a time the new way will be second nature."

Unless she gave it up, Martha thought. Could Aurora hear that?

The sun had topped the trees and was beginning to warm the courtyard around the pool. Martha waited for Aurora to tell her why she had been called.

"Do you remember what I told you in the hut that first day?" Aurora asked. "There is a gossamer veil between the worlds that blows open for some of us?"

"Yes," Martha said. "Now that you mention it, I do."

"You have arrived at this place that is called walking between the worlds."

"I know about that but what does it mean?" It was so early in the morning that Martha didn't know if she was ready for this conversation. But she knew that Aurora did not engage in small talk. She never just sat and chit chatted about the day or her life or what anyone was doing. She never said anything that wasn't important.

"I know it's early," Aurora said, listening to her thoughts again. "Dawn is a good time to have this discussion. Dawn is a time when it's obvious there is more than one world, at least as we know it and commonly accept it to be. The light is coming in to move the shadows; that is what you will be doing. Moving what normally doesn't move, at least in people's perception, but moving it in a natural way. You will bring light into the shadows in people, and as the shadows move inside them, they will see illuminated areas that had been dark before. As they see those areas, their awareness will change. This is part of your gift."

"And part of my responsibility?"

"It will no longer feel like a responsibility," Aurora said. "It is a part of you now. You will find that people want to know. They are looking for tools they can use to understand who they are."

Martha couldn't bring herself to tell Aurora her news. "How do I do this?"

"There's nothing to do. Simply be yourself. It will be a natural outcome of your interactions with others. It is part of the way the world is changing, part of the way we are relearning to be who we once were. It is the way we will all move toward cocreation. It is the way we will transition and thrive."

As Martha thought about this, Aurora poured more tea for both of them. "But that is not why I called you here," she said presently. For some reason, Martha felt a sudden sense of alarm. She remembered Aurora's comment that first day in the hut about having chosen a risky but necessary path. She felt as if the moment was upon her to learn exactly what that meant. It was time for her to speak.

"I can see you feel some alarm," Aurora said, her voice soothing and calm. "I sense that you are concerned about risk."

"Yes," Martha said. "I am at that age where I don't feel as if I have to do risky things anymore. When I can take it easy and enjoy the fruits of my labor. If I don't want to go whitewater rafting or hang-gliding, or do anything that's dangerous, that's my choice."

"I see," Aurora said, and she grew quiet. Martha waited, wondering if she had spoken too quickly. Presently Aurora leaned forward in her chair. "Perhaps there has been a mistake. I remember you mentioned that on the first day." She was silent for a moment, and when she spoke again her voice was calm. "All I will ask is that you return the amulet. It must go to someone in the lineage."

Martha hadn't even said the words, but of course, Aurora knew what she was thinking. Slowly, she took it off. She held it in her hand for a moment, watching the energy inside swirl. Several turquoise orbs moved across the center. She had never noticed them before. The piece seemed to pulse in her palm, and she felt as if she were giving up a part of herself. She held it out to Aurora, who took it and carefully placed it in a pouch around her neck.

Then Martha handed her the book, too.

"I knew the book would eventually come back," Aurora told her. "Not many of the Lost Arts are written down. Most of it is an oral tradition, passed from teacher to teacher. But a few things, over the years, have been recorded in books, for fear the information would be lost. There is always that concern." She put it on the chair next to her. "I am glad you are the one to bring it," she added.

Questions swirled inside Martha's head about the book. Aurora obviously recognized it. Why was that? Where had she seen it? How had Henry gotten it? But as Aurora stood to say goodbye, there was no time to ask. "You'll be able to get home through the portal, but then that's it," Aurora told her. "I would recommend you not use it after that. It won't be safe."

Martha felt a sense of relief, but she was sad to be leaving the school and the people she had met there. "Will I see you again?"

"No. Once you go, our paths will not cross. But I am glad to have met you and I wish you well in your life." Aurora held out her hands. "Goodbye now."

No one else was around today. Save for Aurora, there was no one else for Martha to say goodbye to. As she moved toward the portal, Aurora stopped her.

"You're not the first to leave," she said. "Henry Hocket left several years ago. He thought there was an easier way."

Martha was stunned. "Henry was here?"

"Yes. He was a student here many years ago. He too had promise, but he was impatient. He took the book from the library, thinking if he had that, he could work on his own. He too had been given a feather, but once he turned to the dark arts, he lost it. The feathers will not stay with those who misuse them. He has spent all these years trying to get another."

"How did he manage to get this one?"

"He never had it. He only thought he had it," Aurora replied.

"I'm not sure I'm following you." But at that moment the sky darkened and began to rumble.

Aurora looked up, then turned to Martha. "You must go at once. Hurry."

Martha moved to the central courtyard, took one last look around, and stepped into the portal. She was home in the wink of an eye. It was still early, and the sun was just coming up. For a second, she felt disoriented, because she had already experienced dawn a short time earlier. But the memory of that dawn soon began to fade, as if it hadn't happened. She suddenly realized that once it faded, she would no longer remember it. She reached for her journal and began to write down what had happened. She had gone through the portal, met with Aurora, and they had talked about…she already had forgotten. She put her hand up to touch the amulet. It was gone! That was it, she had given it back. She had been asked to give it back. But why? She struggled to remember. Oh, the risk! That was it. She hadn't even waited to hear what the risk was. She wondered where Chaco was. Perhaps he was in the garden. She really wanted to take a nap. Sleepiness seemed to pull at her, and finally she stretched out on the couch. She would take a short nap, and afterwards….

Martha awoke to an insistent ringing. She was so stiff she could barely move, and by the time she got to the phone, it had stopped ringing. She hadn't been this achy in ages, and she reached in the cupboard for some aspirin.

A bit later, the phone rang again. It was Ned. "Where have you been? I've been trying to reach you for two days."

"I was gone for a few minutes," Martha said. "Other than that I've been right here."

"I'm coming over," he said.

She opened the door when he knocked, and he handed her two newspapers. "Yesterday and today. What's up? Are you all right?"

Frowning, Martha studied the two papers.

"I knew something was up," Ned said, "when you didn't bring in the paper."

Martha didn't know what to say. If what he said was true, she had lost a whole day.

"Sit down," Ned said. "We'll get to the bottom of this. What's the last thing you remember?"

"I don't know. I felt sleepy. I was writing in my journal and I decided to take a nap." The journal was on the floor next to the couch and Ned picked it up.

"Here," he said, handing it to her. "I don't want to read it. But see what you were writing. See if it's applicable."

Martha opened the journal and looked to see what she had written in her last entry, but it didn't make much sense to her. "It says, 'I slipped through the portal to meet with Aurora. She asked for the amulet back. I was afraid to take any more risk, but I didn't even ask what the risk was.' Who is Aurora? And what is this part about the portal?"

Ned stared at her. "What have you done?" he asked in disbelief.

"What do you mean?"

"Where is the amulet?"

"What amulet?"

"The one you've been wearing ever since I met you."

Martha gave him a puzzled look. "I really don't know anything about it," she finally said. He looked genuinely upset.

"Do you remember anything? Do you remember flying?"

Martha gave him a blank stare. "Could you be a little more specific?"

"When I first met you, you took me flying over the river. I said I had always wanted to fly like a bird, and the next thing I knew, you were helping me."

"You have to be kidding me," she said. "I can't fly."

But he was insistent. Martha couldn't believe what she was hearing.

"Do you remember meeting me?" Ned said, suddenly growing concerned.

"Of course I do. We went to eat at Inn on the River. Carol was afraid you wouldn't like the food. We sat outside, and you thought it was a pretty spot."

"And when Joe and Carol ordered dessert, you and I went for a walk."

"I do remember that," Martha said.

"And then we flew. We almost crashed because I didn't think it was possible to fly." Martha looked at him for awhile. There was no reason not to believe him, yet his story seemed incredulous. "I can prove it," he said. "Do you remember the slacks you were wearing? They got caught in the brambles when we landed, and they ripped."

"Perhaps we could talk more later," Martha said. "I feel exhausted, as if I need to rest. Maybe if I rest a bit, I'll remember flying." She knew she wouldn't, but she hated to disappoint him. He seemed so convinced it had happened.

After he left, she wandered into the kitchen and made a sandwich. And then, even though it was early, she decided to go to bed. Upstairs, she brushed her teeth and combed her hair, studying her reflection briefly. Was she getting as forgetful as everyone said? She turned her bed down. On a whim, she went to her closet and pulled out the slacks he had mentioned. She found a small tear in the fabric, just as Ned had described, and some brambles stuck to the hem. Still, she found it hard to believe Ned was telling the truth.

She dreamed that night about a cat. It spoke to her, calling her to come, and in her dream this seemed not the least bit unusual. Its message was clear and obvious, and it made sense to her. In fact, she agreed to follow it as it walked into the woods. In the morning she could no longer remember what the cat had wanted. But after all, it was just a dream and it probably didn't mean anything.

Clark brought the children over after breakfast. While they played in the yard, he told her he had something he wanted to talk to her about.

"Can it wait?" she asked. "I was going to weed the garden."

"Leslie and I are concerned that this house is too much for you to manage. We think you'd be happier with something smaller. There's one about a block from us. Think how close you'd be to your grandchildren."

"I'll look at it later," she said, not really paying attention.

"I could drive you past it now," he said. "It's no trouble. In fact, we could call the agent and set something up to see the inside." He called the children and they all climbed in the car. "What do you think?" he asked a few minutes later, pulling up in front of it. "It's in immaculate condition. It's got two bedrooms. Plenty of space." She stared at the small house with its small yard.

"There's not much room for a garden," she said. "And what about my furniture? I'd have to give some of it away." When Clark suggested that she didn't need it all, she said, "There's no fireplace. I like to sit by the fire in the winter."

"Think about it," he said. "You wouldn't have so much upkeep. Why don't you look at it before you decide?"

Martha sighed. "Set something up for later in the week. Now, I have some gardening to do." There, it was done. Having made the decision to see the house, she didn't feel as bad as she thought. Maybe Clark was right. Why had she bought a big house on two acres of land in the first place?

When they got back to her house, Clark dropped them off and went to do errands. Melissa followed her grandmother to the garden and asked where Chaco was.

"Who?"

"The cat, Grandma."

"I don't have a cat, sweetheart."

"Yes, you do." Melissa insisted. "Did you forget? Daddy says you forget things."

"I would know if I had a cat."

Melissa looked crestfallen.

"You do have a cat. Melissa thinks it talks," Matthew said, to be helpful.

Martha suddenly remembered her dream. "It talks? What does it say?"

Matthew rolled his eyes and went to sail a toy boat in the fountain.

Melissa began to dig in the dirt. "It just talks. You know, with words."

"I had a dream about a cat that could talk. In fact, it told me something important and I can't for the life of me remember what it was."

"Was it orange?"

"Yes, as a matter of fact, it was."

"That's Chaco. He taught you how to fly."

Martha grew pensive, remembering that Ned had remarked about her flying also. "Have you ever seen me fly, sweetheart?"

"No. But Chaco told me you did. He knows everything. You went to school to learn everything too. A school for grown-ups."

Something stirred inside Martha, something familiar. She couldn't put her finger on it, but she knew it was there. "I wonder where we can find Chaco."

"We can call him." She ran around the garden calling the cat's name. Martha went into the kitchen to fix some tea. She looked in the cupboard and found a bag of something called Celestial Citrus. It sounded good, and she put the teabag in her cup and poured boiling water over it. The aroma was wonderful.

Matthew came in from the garden. "Grandma, look!" He held out a green feather.

"Where on earth did you find that?"

"In the garden. It's just like the one you lost."

Martha didn't remember, but she was reluctant to admit to any more forgetfulness. She held it and examined its brilliant hues. She also took a sip of her tea. Suddenly she remembered that she had had a feather like that. What had happened to it? "Matthew, tell me about the feather." Matthew was delighted to be consulted, and he told about finding a feather in the garden and taking it home with him. "And then that man took it and didn't want to give it back."

"Who, dear?"

"He teaches at my dad's college."

After the grandchildren were gone, Martha drank another cup of tea. Feeling significantly revived, she wandered back out to the garden. A butterfly flitted past. She sat down in the chair by the fountain. It seemed like she had lost something important, as if part of her life was missing. Had she really flown? That was an impossible stretch.

An iguana suddenly appeared and stretched out in the sun nearby. "My goodness," she said, "where did you come from?"

"I stop by now and then," it replied. She stared in disbelief. She had always talked to animals. She had just never had one talk to her. "You don't remember me, do you?"

Martha had to admit she didn't.

"I was here not that long ago." It settled in a sunny spot and closed its eyes. "I came by to cheer you up."

"I definitely need cheering up," she said. "But how would you know that?"

"I can sense it. You're one of us. Or at least you used to be."

"What on earth do you mean?"

'You can communicate with us. With all animals. The way humans used to be able to do. They've forgotten how, so when we meet one who can, we like to visit."

"I feel like I've lost something important in my life," Martha ventured.

"Oh, indeed," the iguana said. "But that's what you wanted. We don't know why. Humans often make the choice to limit themselves to small lives, to see only a little bit of the possibility that's out there."

"How did you get here?"

"Same way as always," it said. "Through the portal over there."

"Have you seen the cat named Chaco?"

"I've seen him. I don't know where he is right now. He comes and goes."

"How does the portal work?" Martha asked. "Can you show me?"

"You just step in and go where you want to go. If you don't mind, I'm going to have a siesta."

"Good idea," Martha said, closing her eyes as well. The gardening could wait. She was very sleepy and the stiffness made her want to sit.

Ned woke her up a bit later. "Would you like to go for ice cream?"

"Sit down," she said. She looked him straight in the eye. She was taking a risk, but she needed to do it for her own peace of mind. "I want you to tell me everything you know about me and what I've done since you met me. Something's going on and I need to get to the bottom of it."

18

Martha was astonished by everything Ned told her. Flying, it turns out, was the least of it. A nearly extinct bird had come to her in a dream and then later, after she stepped through a portal and ended up in a rainforest, it had given her a feather, sending her on a path of discovery and empowerment. She had gone to the Ancient Wisdom School in Mexico to take classes to develop her inherent gifts. As Ned talked, Martha realized he didn't have any reason to make up such stories, but still, why wouldn't she remember them? She did remember Ned telling her that he was a man of science, and what he was claiming now seemed to contradict what she knew of him.

"You're the one who showed me that all this was possible," he said. "We have to get to the bottom of this, like you said. You haven't lost all your memories, only the ones pertaining to your new life."

When he said that, she remembered the reader in the market telling her something to that effect, that she was going to have a bigger life. As she decided that she would like to find out what was going on, Ned told her about getting lost in another dimension and her battle with the professor. For some reason, it made her afraid.

"We escaped and then you forgot everything that had happened," Ned finished.

"This sounds far-fetched," Martha said, feeling on edge. "It's like something you would read in a book. I am not sure I want to be in a battle with anyone."

"You're starting to remind me of myself," Ned said.

They looked at each other for a moment while Martha debated about what to do.

"I was not a believer," Ned admitted. "You told me I needed to believe or we'd get in trouble. I just followed your instructions."

"That doesn't sound like me," Martha said.

"I didn't know you before," Ned said. "All I know is that I was impressed by your courage and adventurousness. I'd never met anyone like you. You were filled with a zest for life. It was contagious. I wanted to be a part of it."

"Why can't I remember?"

"Maybe Henry put a spell on you." It was a long shot, and Ned knew it. But Martha wouldn't hear of it. Ned was ready to give up.

Martha shook her head. "There has to be an explanation," she admitted. "For the life of me, I don't know what it is."

"I remember when we were in the cave, you went back in time to figure out how to escape. Perhaps you could do that again."

She mulled over the idea. "I don't have a clue how to begin," she finally said. "I wish I knew what was going on."

"All I know is you've changed," Ned said. "It's like the life has gone out of you. You were so dynamic. You were powerful. You were doing all kinds of things. Lately all you've done is sit."

"I feel quite tired," she said.

"You made me come to life," he continued. "I was just going through the motions when I met you. Nothing really mattered. I felt discouraged and I'd given up hope. You made me see life in a new way. You made me want to live. We have to get those feelings back for you."

They heard someone coming and turned to see Angela. "Martha! I thought I'd pop in for a visit. How's everything?"

"Not good," Ned said. "Martha seems to have forgotten everything she learned."

Angela frowned and pulled a chair over. "This is unfortunate news," she said. "Have you talked to Aurora?"

Martha looked confused. "No, who is that? Ned mentioned her, too."

Angela looked at Ned, who shrugged. She quickly considered her options. "I'm going to talk to Aurora," she said after a moment. "I'll be back as soon as I can. Wait here."

Martha went inside to make lemonade, and Ned waited by the fountain, wracking his brain. Why couldn't Martha remember? It didn't make sense. He listened to the water cascading down the fountain. For a second, he thought it was actually talking to him, encouraging him to listen to what he knew was true. He strained to make sense of it, but finally decided it was just the usual sound of water.

A few minutes later, Angela reappeared. "I have bad news," she told him, sitting down. "Martha told Aurora she was quitting. She felt it was too dangerous. She gave the amulet back. Aurora told her she would forget what she had learned. The powers are only available to those who use them."

Ned was shocked. "She chose this? I wish she had talked to me about it."

"Me too," Angela said. "There has to be something we can do. Let me think about it. She was a natural. That's not something you can just walk away from. Don't tell her what I just told you," she whispered as Martha came out carrying a tray filled with glasses and a pitcher of fresh-squeezed lemonade. "At least not until we figure out what to do."

"So," Martha said, serving everyone, "shall we play a game of cribbage?"

At that moment, Sheila arrived, toting a box. She greeted everyone and was surprised to find Angela there. "I didn't know I'd get to see you, too," she said. "Here, help me with this." The two carried the box and put it down in front of Martha.

"Open it," Sheila instructed.

Martha took the lid off the box to reveal a small sculpture of a dancing figure who was half woman, half jaguar. "Oh my, what is it?"

"It's you. Remember the dance of transformation you did when you learned to walk between the worlds?"

Martha looked at her wide-eyed.

"She doesn't re—" Ned started to say, but Martha interrupted. "The dance. Yes. Thank you, it's lovely."

Angela pulled Sheila aside while Ned admired the sculpture with Martha. They talked for a minute and then returned. When her phone rang, Martha went to answer it in the kitchen. "We have to do something," Angela said. "I say we take her to the bonfire Steven is hosting tonight. It will be dark enough that I don't think anyone will notice. We'll tuck her hair inside a baseball cap. We have to make her realize that she made a mistake by dropping out. What do you think? Once she sees her mistake she can talk to Aurora."

"I'm in," Sheila said. They both looked at Ned.

"Count me in," he said. "What time?"

"We'll go to my house for dinner," Sheila said. "We can get ready there. Why don't you go get whatever you need." Ned was gone in a flash.

Martha returned and sat down with Angela and Sheila. "Clark is coming by now to take me to see the new house. He managed to set up an appointment today. I'm going to go get ready. Afterwards, they're taking me out for dinner. Thank you both for coming, and I hope I see you soon. Oh, Ned's gone," she said, sounding disappointed as she looked around. "If he comes back before you go, tell him I had to go out."

"Now what?" Angela asked, following Sheila into the house to put the sculpture on the coffee table. "Do we wait or do we go for it?" They were plotting as they looked at each other, and the same idea seemed to occur to both of them at the same time.

"I say we go for it, before it's too late."

"Exactly my thinking."

They both called to Martha. She came down the stairs, surprised to still see them there. "I thought you'd be gone. Perhaps you'd like to come along and see the house."

"Actually, we have a surprise for you. We're taking you somewhere."

"What for?" She seemed puzzled.

"We can't tell you," Sheila said. "But we promised we'd get you there."

"But Clark is on his way here."

Sheila took her hand and led her out to the garden. Ned had just returned. "What do you know about this?" Martha asked. Angela wrote a note and left it for Clark, then hurried outside.

"Just along for the ride," he answered. Sheila motioned for him to take Martha's other hand.

They heard a car door slam in the driveway, signaling that Clark had arrived. "Mom? Let's go," he called, heading to the house.

"Quickly," Angela said. "Everybody hold on." They made their way to the portal.

When Clark went into the house, all he found was a quickly scribbled note on the kitchen counter. "Gone to a surprise party," it read. "See you soon."

The Tucson evening was warm and the air was fragrant. Martha sat on Sheila's patio, enjoying a margarita. "This is more fun than looking at a silly house," she said. Besides, why do I need to move? And why does Clark keep bringing it up? It's my life."

"Now you're talking," Ned said, encouraged to see her feeling happier. He was barbecuing chicken while Sheila tossed a salad.

"More chips?" Angela asked, passing the basket. The sun was sinking on the horizon, triggering a memory. "Remember what Steven told us about the sunset that first night? It's a time of transition, when we're moving into darkness and dreamtime."

"That's right. He said there is no separation between the worlds at sunset."

"It's a point of entry," Angela said. "We're going to study that soon."

"Martha and I went somewhere," Ned said. He turned to her. "Do you know where that was?" She shook her head. "It was like we were on the other side of everything, looking in," he continued. "Only we couldn't be seen."

"So you did it," Sheila said. "I knew you'd figure it out. You walked between the worlds." They ate dinner and talked as the sun sank lower. "If we're going to get to Steven's dreamtime celebration on time, we need to get moving. It starts at sunset." She found a sweatshirt and a baseball cap for Martha to wear.

"We're going to a surprise party?" she asked.

"Let's just say you're the surprise guest," Sheila told her as the four of them stepped into the portal again.

An enormous bonfire was blazing when they arrived, sending sparks into the night sky. Students milled in small groups around the fire. Ned stood with the three women, watching the flames shoot into the darkness, nervously wondering what the night held. He kept an eye on Martha as Sheila went to see who else was there. "I don't see Aurora," she said, returning. "Just Steven. He's across the way. There are quite a few people here, even Roger. He's nervous as ever."

"I've been here before," Martha said, looking around and suddenly getting a sense of familiar surroundings.

"Yes, when you came to school," Angela said. "We brought you here hoping you would want to be a part of this again."

"We want you to come back to the classes," Sheila added. "We miss you. It's not the same."

"I'm remembering bits and pieces," Martha said. "The energy here is amazing. I have a sense of connection, as if I am a part of everything."

"You are," Sheila said. "That's what this is about."

Martha decided to stroll around before the ceremony began, and Sheila walked with her. Angela stayed with Ned. "It's better that neither one of you is alone," Sheila said. "There is tremendous power at an event like this, because many beings come to experience and take part in the exchange." After a time, Martha began to feel energized and alive. "I had forgotten what this was like," she said. "I am not sure why I decided to quit."

"I don't know either," Sheila admitted.

But in spite of her renewed sense of vitality, an edgy uneasiness dogged her. She found herself looking over her shoulder.

"What's wrong?" Sheila asked.

"Something's not right," Martha said. Sheila looked around, too, but saw nothing. Soon they found Ned and Angela again.

"I think I'd like to take some classes," Ned said, getting caught up in the energy created by the event. "This is like nothing I've ever experienced, yet it feels oddly familiar. I have an enormous sense of well-being."

"It awakens something inside you that's been dormant," Angela explained. "It's your inner knowing, which you probably have underutilized in your life."

"I really like that portal thing," he added. "Beats the heck out of airplanes."

Henry watched Martha from the shadows. He had spotted his archenemy almost immediately, moments after she arrived. He was chafing. He thought she was out of the picture. Why was she here? It was the only wrench in his plans. He was growing increasingly agitated.

He circled over to Mallow, who had helped him in the cave.

"Why so jumpy?" Mallow asked.

Henry gestured with his head and Mallow's gaze followed. "Who is it?"

"That Martha woman. Why is she here?"

"I thought she had gone back to vegetating in Seaport. Who's with her?"

"Current students." Henry stared at the foursome for a moment, turning suddenly as Martha looked his way. "Did she see me?"

"No." Mallow shifted uncomfortably.

"I think she senses something. The plan will still work, but we need to act quickly."

"I think it's better to wait," Mallow argued. "In a few minutes, everyone will be dancing into the dream. It will be easy then."

"Time is of the essence. I didn't plan for her to be here. I need to act before she gets wind. She is the only person who can stop us."

A sudden sound caught everyone off guard. Steven had hit a large gong, and the soothing tone resonated through the gathering, getting their attention. "We are ready," Steven announced. A second sound, like thunder, began to grow, and soon it became clear it was drumming. "We are calling in the powers," Steven said, his voice clear and loud. "At the moment of sunset, we held the opening for all to enter the dreamtime. You have been preparing as you stood by the fire, and we will all be ushered in now by the dreamtime spirits. Remember that everything is real. Be clear with your intention in order to follow it through dreamtime, and any questions that you have will be answered by the dreamtime spirits. This is a life-changing experience, because anything that has held you back in your life can be let go. You can recapture lost power and reclaim lost dreams. You can literally change your life, and emerge as the person you have dreamed of becoming. Now follow me."

One by one they stepped into the dreamtime opening. Sheila held onto Martha, and Angela held onto Ned. "We'll stay together if we can," Sheila said. "Make it part of your intention."

Right behind them were Henry and Mallow. "We'll take care of her first," Henry whispered. "Then it's all ours."

"It better be," Mallow hissed. "Because you promised this would happen weeks ago, and I'm running out of patience."

"Whatever you do, stay with me."

As she entered the dreamtime, Martha was overcome with a sense of urgency, as if there was something she needed to do. Her intention to stay with the others faded in the face of this new feeling. Yes, there was something she needed to do, and she had always known it, from the time she was small. She needed to know herself and her own ability, and she needed to surrender to the guidance that was calling to her, pulling her, pushing her, leading her. It was the most powerful force she had ever felt, and yet she was unafraid. She melded with it, as she had melded with the first stirrings deep within her that day in the rainforest when all this had begun. She felt something at her side. The others had vanished, but something familiar brushed against her. She was moving too fast to tell what it was. She was almost flying. The world was intensely beautiful— there were bright green grasses beneath her and a liquid blue sky above.

The memories flooded in like a sneaker wave—the bird in her dream, flying along the river with Ned, Aurora entrusting her with the amulet, going to the school. And the dance of transformation. With a sudden clarity that almost took her breath away, she remembered the moment of embracing her true power. Simultaneously, she had entered the world of interrelationship and inherent knowing. At that moment she had known who she was, without a shadow of doubt, and she had been intimately connected to everything else that lived and breathed and shared the world with her. It was enormously satisfying and safe, and it seemed to her that that was the way it should be.

But she had let someone make her afraid. She had given her power to the fear and let it move her in a direction she didn't want to go. To think she had almost given up the world she had discovered right at her doorstep!

She wondered if she had just found it by accident. Or—and this is what a voice inside was telling her—perhaps by following her dream, she had created a world of empowerment and acceptance. By listening to what she wanted for the first time in her life, she had discovered a magical mysterious universe that embraced her the moment she opened to it. It had always been there, just out of her line of vision, a huge, magnificent untapped resource, as stunning and alive as the amulet Aurora had given her. And she, for whatever reason, had given it back.

There was a question dogging her, straining for consciousness. What was it? She pulled it into her awareness, and it startled her. *Why are you afraid?* She wasn't afraid, she told herself. Flying was easy, it was natural. She could do it with no problem. Why should she be afraid?

But as the question tugged insistently at her awareness, she focused on it. It captured her attention. Her perception narrowed, and her margin for error increased. As the question buzzed in her head, she was no longer open to perceiving what was around her. Steven had warned them: *You are entering the unknown. Be alert to danger. Let the secrets of the unknown reveal themselves to you and guide you. What you gather will nourish the seeds of your inner wisdom, and you will feel it grow inside you. Focus your attention on your dream.*

But all she could feel was fear, gnawing at her under her skin, chewing on her confidence, ripping off whole chunks of her courage, eating her alive and making her small.

At that moment, she flew into what felt like a net. As she struggled vainly to free herself, she saw someone looking at her. She struggled with all her might to break free, and she heard a wicked laugh. "This time I've got you," Hocket said, his voice dripping with malice. "Mallow!" he called, and another man tied the net. "You won't be escaping this time. I'll see to that."

Her dream had suddenly become a nightmare. She fought against the net, and tried to push back the fear that gripped her even more profoundly.

"You weren't supposed to be here," Hocket said. "You could have lived a quiet life in Seaport. But you had to interfere with my plans. This time you'll pay." Martha worked to escape, pulling at the net and the ropes. He watched her with interest. "It's no use.

You might as well give up." The two men dragged her to a cave and pulled her inside. And then they left.

Alone in the dark, Martha called for help. The walls of the cave began to collapse around her, and she found it hard to get her breath. Her fear turned to panic. How had this happened? Why hadn't she stayed home to live in the little house that Clark had picked out for her?

The darkness overwhelmed her. Her struggle slowed, until she was moving in slow motion. She felt like she was swimming in molasses, as if every motion took all the strength she had. She wasn't cut out for this.

That was it! That was why she quit! Now she remembered with a clarity that surprised her. She remembered her fear when she had faced this man—Henry—before. How could she escape? What if she didn't? What if, as he said, there was no escaping this time?

All the fears she had ever felt descended on her. They seemed to be attacking her from all directions, taunting her. She struggled against them, and she struggled against the net. Finally she realized it was hopeless. No one would find her here. No one would ever know what happened to her. Everything she had wanted would end in this dark cave because of a man who was threatened by her search for her own power. Martha began to cry. She had come so close to discovering her true self, to reclaiming her lost dream, to reinventing her life. Like the reader said, she had come to the doorway of opportunity.

19

Hocket moved quickly. "Keep up, keep up," he urged Mallow. "I can't guarantee your safety if you fall behind." It bothered him that Mallow was lagging; he was growing tired of checking on him. He needed to focus on the tasks at hand. "The hardest part is over," he said, talking more to himself than his companion, who was barely within earshot. "The dream is within reach. I will have the power I wanted when I left that school. Keep up," he snapped at Mallow. "You won't know where to go without me."

He was following the others through dreamtime, watching their dreams, waiting for the opportunity to make his move. His vigilance was key. It was his foot in the door. There would be openings, and he would be there to take advantage of them.

His plan was going better than he had imagined. Capturing Martha was a coup. This time, he knew, she would not escape. She would no longer be a thorn in his side. He felt only a slight tinge of regret. After all, she had made it possible for him to have the coveted feather for a short time. He would never have imagined it would fall into his hands so easily. It put his plan into action sooner than he thought would be possible. With her out of the way, it would be his.

All that remained for him now, as he worked his way through dreamtime, was to trick the others into giving up their power through their fears and weaknesses. He had done it before, he would do it now. He knew what he wanted and he planned to get it.

The fact that people were used to giving up their power to others made it easy for someone like him to operate. When he first went to the school many years ago, he decided it would be much faster to take advantage of other people than to sit through the classes. Even if he studied the lost arts, it would take dedication on his part to acquire personal power. He finally realized he wanted more than personal power, he wanted control over others. The only way to get that was to take their power away. He imagined that control would feel like personal power. He believed it would give him the sense of power that he craved, even if it wasn't authentic power.

He studied the group Martha was with. They seemed to be good friends. That fueled his anger, because he had never had many friends. He was jealous of those who made friends easily, and jealous when he wasn't liked as well as he imagined others were. In part, he had concocted this plan in order to gain the admiration of others. If he had to destroy a few people in the process, so be it. The end result he pictured was that people would like him. They would have to like him, or he would destroy them. "Keep up or else!" he shouted impatiently, beginning to lose sight of Mallow. He hesitated momentarily, trying to keep the others in view as he tried to hurry his companion. But he knew he couldn't wait, it would ruin his plan.

Someone bumped into him from above, and he ducked. He was dismayed to see it was that slow student, the one who seemed to take longer to learn than the rest. He was in over his head, and Hocket was sorry to see him here. Just stay out of my way, Hocket thought.

He wanted nothing to stop his plan, which he felt was pure genius. Through trial and error, he had discovered that when people were afraid of something irrational, they gave up their power more easily. Fear was a good distraction, as it made people focus on what they lacked instead of what they had. Then he simply took their power to use for himself. He liked to keep Mallow afraid, because it made him submissive. He needed an assistant who wouldn't challenge him.

Speaking of which, where was he? When Hocket looked this time, Mallow had disappeared. He debated for a brief second about whether to go back for him or push on. But there wasn't really a choice. Already the others were drifting out of sight. He couldn't lose track of them because he was in unfamiliar territory, and he was navigating by tailing. If he had no one to follow, he might get lost himself.

Steven, meanwhile, had just had a disturbing message from a Teller: Martha was there. "Are you sure? She was cautioned not to use the portals."

"Sheila and Angela brought her. Sheila told Ned they were going to the bonfire."

"Who's Ned?"

"He wants to take classes."

Steven was suddenly worried. There were people in dreamtime who weren't supposed to be there. They didn't have the skills to navigate through. He'd never encountered a problem like this before. There was no way to get help, or to check on those who were there without permission.

"Hocket was upset to see Martha," the Teller said before flying off.

"Hocket! He's here too?" The fact that Hocket was in dreamtime made him pause. Hocket had tried for years to infiltrate the school to steal power from those who acquired it. But he had never entered a dreamtime. Steven needed to act.

Since he was leading the students through dreamtime, he had to continue doing that so that no one got lost. If he turned around and went back to provide help, he would create a mess. Some students might be lost, unable to find their way out. He quickly considered his options.

Clark, meanwhile, reported to Leslie that his mother was gone again. "She was supposed to go look at the new house. I wonder what's up," he said, frowning. "There was a note about a surprise party."

"Maybe one of her friends is having a birthday," Leslie said. "I'm sure she's OK. You know how unpredictable she's been lately, doing whatever she feels like."

"It's not like her," he said. "Lately she's not herself."

"Maybe she can see the new house tomorrow." Leslie was busy making dinner, and she didn't want to be interrupted. "Why don't you check on the children?"

"I went ahead and told the agent to list her house. We'll never get her out of there if we wait for her to decide."

"Do you think she'll be upset?" She began to set the table.

"Nothing I can't handle," he said. "She's been kind of quiet the last few days. I think she'll take it OK."

"I don't know why she bought that house in the first place. It's way too big for her. She's been so independent lately. It was making the kids a little too independent."

"You mean like when they snuck out on the babysitter? Here, do you want some help?" He distributed the forks and knives.

"We're lucky something didn't happen to them. What will you do about the cat?"

"It hasn't been around lately. It may have wandered off."

"Dinner's almost ready. Have the kids wash their hands."

"Matthew. Melissa. Time for dinner." Clark switched the television on to see if there was any news. Then he went to help carry the food to the table.

"Where's Grandma?" Melissa asked, coming in from outside. "I thought she was having dinner, too."

"She went to a party," her father said. "Something came up."

"Did she fly there?" Melissa asked.

"Of course not," Leslie said. "Sit down, the food's getting cold. Matthew, now!" They sat down to eat as Matthew bounded down the stairs.

"Is Chaco there?" Melissa asked, but no one heard her. They were paying attention to a news report that Henry Hocket, a science professor at the college, was missing. He had not shown up in the last week to teach any of his classes at the college. No one had seen him in five days.

"Ned's gone to a party with Martha," Carol told Joe. "He left a note. He won't be here for dinner."

"He's certainly having himself a time," Joe said. "Little did we know, huh?" He winked at Carol, who ignored him. She was spooning beef stew onto two plates.

"I know you're amused by it. If he gets involved with her, he won't have much time for me." She put his plate down on the table. "I made this stew for him," she noted, as if that added insult to the injury.

"He might end up living right next door. You'll be able to see him every day. You can't ask for more than that." He put his paper napkin on his lap. "Besides, he had the stew last night. This is left over."

"I don't know if she's the person I would choose for him," Carol said indignantly, smoothing her own napkin.

"It's not your choice," Joe reminded her. "He's smiling again. Leave him be."

Aurora and Olivia had gone out for dinner in the City of Eternal Spring. They were seated outdoors in a restaurant courtyard, having a glass of wine. "It's almost as peaceful here as at the school," Aurora said. "I like coming here."

Water cascaded down a fountain in the center of the courtyard, and a rainbow of lush bougainvillea and hibiscus surrounded them. "How do you think Steven's dreamtime event is going?" Olivia wondered out loud.

"He's accomplished at leading them," Aurora responded, leaning back in her chair and enjoying the surroundings. "And he's a gifted teacher. Students come out of the experience transformed. They are new people. Certainly their visions are strong and they are able to move forward with greater power after the experience. I'm sorry Martha quit before she was able to go through the dreamtime. Had she done that, I think she would have stayed. She would have…." Her voice trailed off.

"Go ahead, finish, it's good to acknowledge it. Then we can move on."

"You know as well as I, she would have been our best student yet. Certainly our most powerful. It is not often I see someone with her ability."

"That was a remarkable day when she found you in the hut," Olivia said. "I can still remember your excitement when you came back to the school. I didn't know what had happened."

"We knew someone was coming. We just didn't know who or when. Actually she was lucky to catch me there. I had gone to collect herbs. I hadn't been there in several weeks. The timing was perfect. It surprised even me."

"It all works out exactly like it's supposed to."

"Yes, and the perfection of it can be sublimely beautiful. That is what brings me joy, to experience that moment of precision in what looks like haphazard chaos. When I realized what was happening…when the awareness of it penetrated…." She grew silent, remembering.

"It's definitely chaos, but perhaps not haphazard. But yes, the moments when the orchestration is perfect makes everything worthwhile."

Aurora laughed, feeling a sensation of delight. They were in no rush tonight, and they were enjoying their evening away from the responsibilities of the school. "She was so baffled by what had happened. She felt it was a terrible mistake. She kept telling me that she was just standing in a house she wanted to buy and asking how she could get back there."

Olivia studied her. "I haven't asked you this before, but did it ever cross your mind that perhaps it was a mistake?"

"No." Aurora looked at her from across the table. "Do you know why?"

Olivia, suddenly curious, raised her eyebrows. This was a story she hadn't heard.

"Because the quetzal told us almost nothing about her. He wanted us to have no preconceptions. All he said was, be ready for the one with the feather. When she knocked on the door of the hut, I thought she was a tourist, hopelessly lost from one of those expeditions that goes by looking for the Lost City. She looked dehydrated so I invited her in for tea."

"They pay good money for those trips," Olivia said. "And they never find it. All they see are the nearby ruins."

"I was prepared to call Clemente to bring the burro around," Aurora continued, "when I noticed the feather. She was carrying it in her hand, ever so casually. I almost didn't see it." Aurora picked up a *bollito* and broke it in half. "That is how I knew."

"I had no idea. I knew you knew, and I had complete faith in that." Olivia leaned back in her chair. "It still surprises me that she dreamed about the quetzal."

"I don't think she realizes even yet how unusual her dream was. But he called her to give her the feather. She chose to accept his call by stepping through the portal."

"And then he sent her to you."

"Yes. It was perfect." Aurora smiled at the memory.

"So what now?" Olivia asked.

Aurora shook her head. Their food came and they spent a few moments admiring the presentation and enjoying the aroma of garlic and spices before they began to eat. After a time Olive spoke again. "To think her ability was hidden all those years. How is that possible? At the very least, she must have felt a vague dissatisfaction with life, wouldn't you think? Like there was something missing?"

"She spoke to me about it briefly," Aurora said. "How is your food? Mine is wonderful, as always." Olivia nodded in agreement. "She said that she had lived for her husband and her family, never for herself. And she was quite lonely after her husband died, because her son was involved with work and his own family. She began to have regrets about never having pursued some of her own dreams. I know when she was at the school that she began to develop a sense of who she was." Aurora stared into the distance. "And I know she was forever changed by the Dance of the Jaguar. She knows it, and the animals know it. I do not think they will let her forget."

"The thing now is, who will the amulet go to?" Olivia's question was to the point. "No one has shown up in her absence. The lineage will be broken. It was so clearly hers. She was the quetzal's choice." Both women were silent for a moment.

"You know what I am thinking," Aurora said. "That perhaps the lineage ends. It almost ended when Quetzalcoatl left the city. But it has endured. We will continue to teach it as long as we can."

"Would it mean the end of the school?" Olivia stopped eating. Her face grew serious.

"I think we should enjoy this delicious dinner," Aurora said, "and not spoil it with what might be. It is never good to jump into expectation or projection. It is not up to us."

"But what would happen in the world?" Olivia said. "What would happen if we were no longer teaching students and passing on the ancient arts? When I think of how much good they have done...." She didn't finish her sentence.

"We shouldn't think about that now," Aurora said. "The tradition has survived for thousands of years, through great challenges, always bringing new students into the teaching and sending new light into the world. We have had a great beneficial impact on the history of humankind, despite the fact that there is little awareness of it. By teaching the skills, we increase creative cooperation in the human realm. We have to continue to do this work so that there is less dissension and fighting, so that war as a solution becomes a thing of the past. If the tradition were not to continue…I don't even want to think how the world would change."

Olivia shook her head. "Nor do I." She took a last sip of her wine. "Aurora."

Aurora looked at her, sensing what she was going to say.

"I wonder if…."

"What?"

"It's just an idea."

'I know what you're thinking. We can't ask Martha to come back. It has to be her choice. It has to come from within. Always, the student initiates the contact. That is how we know who the students are. Otherwise we would not."

"You're right. It was wishful thinking."

"I had the same idea," Aurora confessed. "It's tempting. To see someone like her, and then to lose her."

Dusk settled on the city. In the distance a dog barked. Somewhere, music played. It was a beautiful evening. Aurora, finishing her *pollo con ajo*, felt a vague uneasiness. She couldn't pinpoint what it was, but she had learned to trust her feelings.

"Something is wrong," she said. "Someone is in trouble."

"Then we must go," Olivia said. Moments later, they were on their way back to the school, following the familiar narrow street. "Can you tell who it is?"

"It's Steven," Aurora said. "The lineage is being challenged. It is serious. We must go at once."

20

Martha felt something moving over her. She rubbed her eyes and opened them. She tried to pull her blanket off but she couldn't, and then she realized she was still trapped in the net. She was awake, but her nightmare was real. She heard a raspy voice and strained to see who was talking, but all she saw was a snake. Alarmed, she drew in her breath sharply. She hoped it wasn't going to strike. But it spoke. It took her a moment to understand. "You're trapped," it said. "The way out is to dream."

"What do you mean?"

"Dreaming is the resolution. Dream your way out. If you stay in your fears, you will stay trapped."

"But I am trapped." Martha grabbed the net for emphasis.

"You're stuck in fear because that is all you are thinking. You must use your power to follow your intention out. Make a new dream. Your old dream is done. It brings you nothing but confinement, as you can see."

"Can't you do something?" She could feel her resistance to her own power because she had never learned to use it.

"You have within you everything you need to do this. Hocket used your fear against you. That is how he caught you. It is how he tried to catch you before, and you went back in time and got out, and then you returned to your old life. This time, when you get out, you will be in your new life. That is what you are resisting. That is what you are afraid of."

"How do you know all this?"

Before her eyes, the snake changed into a cat.

"Chaco!" she cried. "I know you can help me."

"No one can help you if you don't help yourself."

She tried to focus on what he said. It was as if the words were just beyond her understanding. "Help me. Cut the net."

"I have no way to cut it," he said. "The dreamtime is yours. You make the dream. I must go. Hocket is trying to take over the dream we all have of freedom."

"Wait!" Martha called. But he had turned into a bird and was gone. She sat there wrapped in nets and rope and tried to remember his words. How could she follow her intention out? Suddenly she saw her intention stretched out like a thread in front of her. It led through the net and out of the cave. If she was tiny, she could easily follow it. But she wasn't small enough to fit through the holes of the net. She stared at her intention, clearly making its way out of the cave. It seemed to glow, as if it were made of light instead of thread. As she watched it, she became focused on its direction. She followed it, moving with the light, through the net, out of the cave. She kept her eyes on it, never wavering. Even when she was out of the cave, she kept her attention on it. It was essential to stay focused. She had never seen it so clearly. At first she felt like she was following it, but after a time she realized she was connected to it. She had become her intention, and once she made it a part of who she was, she no longer needed to stare at it. She was able to follow it intuitively. At that point, she was able to look around to see where she was.

She was in a land of rocks and sand, a desert. She moved quickly over the surface, and soon she was flying. A sense of urgency had come over her again. She was moving toward something. Her fear was gone, but her focus was intense. She needed to find Chaco and the others. She needed to stop Henry.

Where was everyone? Below her she saw something moving. When she flew closer to investigate, she found Sheila, sitting on a rock, crying. "I'm nobody," she said. "Henry told me I'll never be anybody."

The terrain was rough. Martha called on a mountain goat to help. "Sheila," she called. "Henry filled you with fear. You must begin to dream. See your artwork in the gallery and see people responding to it. See them buying it and taking it home. See them looking at it, and finding beauty and meaning. When you've done that, catch up with me." She left the mountain goat with Sheila.

She continued on her way until there were trees and a river. She found Ned straining to paddle upstream in a small boat. "Life is a struggle," he said. "What is the point?"

Martha called on a salmon to help because it knew how to swim both ways. "You're going the wrong way," she told Ned. "Go with the flow and enjoy the ride. There's nothing to it."

"But it's not supposed to be easy," he said. "Henry told me."

"It's whatever you want it to be. Dream a new dream, then catch up with me."

A little further on she found Angela going in circles. "Henry said I never get it right," Angela told her. "I keep trying, and I keep getting it wrong."

Martha called on hummingbird, who could fly faster than Angela's circles. "Angela, it's only your fear," she said. "There is no right or wrong way. Dream the dream you want to live. Then catch up with me. We have to stop Henry. He's spreading fear everywhere. He's poisoning the dream for everyone."

Martha's intention had grown strong and bright. No one else was coming yet, but she felt confident enough to stop Hocket on her own if she had to. She would do whatever it took. All at once she saw him. "Henry," she called. "You've forgotten something important."

"I never forget anything," he cried, coming toward her. "Who helped you get free? Mallow!" He called his partner to assist him, and the two of them rushed toward her.

"You forgot the most important thing of all," she said. Now she called on jaguar to help her with courage, and jaguar swiftly appeared.

"Control is the most important thing, and I'll soon have it all."

"Control is an illusion," she said, remembering her dance of transformation and realizing that everything she needed she had within. "Control is something you think you need because you're not secure enough to let other people be themselves. But control is not real. It's not true. You can't trust it. That is your mistake."

"I've taken control of everyone," he screamed. "I'll soon be in charge. You will all have to listen to me."

"What you forgot," she said, "is the power of every person to dream."

"Then where is everyone?" he challenged. "Dreamtime is almost over, and I don't see anybody dreaming. They're all afraid."

She heard his familiar wicked laugh.

"Grab her," he told Mallow. They ran at her. Martha narrowly escaped by jumping past them with a catlike movement that she had learned in her dance. She was surprised by her grace and agility and speed.

"You're wasting your time," she said. They rushed at her again. She leapt out of the way and the two men collided. "You're acting out of fear right now," she told Henry. "That's why it's futile. You're afraid of not being in control. You're stuck. That's why you can't get me." Again he tried and failed. He was out of breath.

"You won't win," he said. "I will get you eventually."

"Of course I won't win. I'm not competing with you," she said. "I'm simply dreaming my life. And you're not in it." Once more Henry lunged at her, but this time he tripped and collapsed in a heap on top of Mallow just as Sheila, Ned and Angela appeared, each following their intentions. And behind them there were others.

Not far ahead, Steven was waiting with Chaco. As the group of dreamtime participants arrived at their destination, they all began talking at once, telling how they'd gotten stuck in their fears, and how they'd dreamed their way out. For the first time, Roger wasn't last. They gathered around Martha, who reminded them about how they had reclaimed the power they had given to Henry.

Ned asked where Henry was. "He was dreaming about control," Steven said. "But now he's afraid he'll never have it. He got stuck in the fear. And he will stay stuck if he has no power to get out."

The celebration around the bonfire lasted for hours. Each student told a story of transformation, of letting go of fears and becoming more authentic. "A mountain goat spoke to me," Sheila said. "I was lost and afraid, and when I saw it, it told me to challenge my fear. At that moment my fear was released and I felt a sense of power and authenticity. I wish I could explain it better."

"You were stuck in fear," Steven said. "When you let that go, you expanded into who you are now. That is why it feels powerful. You integrated."

Ned tried to stay in the shadows, since he hadn't been invited to the ceremony. "You're a student now," Steven said, turning to address him. "The way we know you are a student is that you arrive. There is no protocol."

Ned was relieved and told his own story of meeting fear. "I was rowing in a river against the current, struggling to make progress, and a fish swam up to me and spoke," he said. "It told me to let go of the struggle. That's when everything changed." He paused, his lips pursed as if he was thinking. "I wouldn't have believed it except that not so long ago I heard an iguana talk at Martha's house." His comment made the others laugh.

It continued like that until everyone had had a chance to relate their story. Martha was last. Just as she began, Aurora and Olivia arrived. "I thought I had forgotten everything," Martha said. "I thought I no longer wanted to discover who I truly was. My friends helped me realize my decision was hasty. It was based on fear. That's why I came here tonight. I wanted to regain what I had lost."

She looked at Aurora before she continued, and Aurora nodded as if she wasn't surprised to see her, even though she was. "I became trapped in my own fear and I thought I would not survive," Martha said. "I was trapped by my beliefs that I was not powerful. A snake came and spoke to me." She looked at Chaco. "It told me I had to help myself, something I have never been willing to do. I have always wanted others to help me, to make my decisions. I was afraid to stand on my own. As soon as I became clear about what I wanted, I was released."

Aurora came over to greet her. "I am so glad you are here," she said. "I have something for you. I have a feeling that this time, it won't be coming back to me." She removed the amulet from around her neck and handed it to Martha. Angela, Sheila, Ned and Steven clapped.

"I accept the responsibility and the gift," Martha said, feeling the familiar warmth of the amulet around her neck. She gestured at Ned. "Meet your newest student. I took the liberty of showing him a few things already." There was good-natured laughter from the group, especially Angela.

"You're a good teacher," Angela said. "I had to learn to be a good listener so that I could overcome my resistance. I see that Ned's not wearing pajamas," she added, recalling her own memorable experience.

"I am not surprised you have begun teaching him already, Martha," Aurora said. "Teachers begin teaching when they are ready. They show up, just like students do. We never advertise or hire."

"I have no idea how to teach," Martha said. Again there was laughter.

"Don't mind her," Angela said to the others. "She never knows how to do anything until she does it. She was using portals before she knew what they were called."

Aurora pulled Martha aside. "It's good that you don't know. That way you'll be open to finding out. If you're open, the energy moves freely through you, and before you know it, you're doing it.

Just like portals. That's what makes a good teacher, not knowing everything."

Ned began to talk to Steven about an upcoming class. A few minutes later Steven announced that the ceremony was ending. The energy began to ebb and as a result people grew tired. Soon they were moving off to their respective homes.

"Martha," Aurora said. "We have news for you. Can you come by the school tomorrow?" She agreed, and then she and Ned said goodbye to Sheila and Angela and stepped into the portal.

"That was quite a night," Ned said when they were back. "I'm exhausted, but I will talk to you in the morning. What do they mean about manifesting chocolate? I didn't have a clue what they were talking about. Are you sure I'm cut out for this?"

"You showed up, didn't you? That's how it works." She waved goodbye and wandered inside. A minute later she was asleep. She didn't dream at all. When she woke up in the morning, her first thought was Clark. She imagined he was upset, and she needed to call him. She went out to get the morning newspaper on the porch, and a FOR SALE sign in her front yard caught her eye. It must be a mistake, she thought, dialing Clark. But Clark knew all about it and asked how soon the agent could show the house.

"Clark, it's not your house to sell. It's mine. I understand your concern, and I appreciate how much you care about me. But I am going to make my own decisions now. I will keep you informed as much as possible, especially if they affect you." She hung up the phone and called Ned. "I need your assistance," she said, "when you have a moment."

"I'm just making arrangements for class," he replied. "I will be right over."

She was pulling the hefty FOR SALE sign out of the ground when he arrived. He helped her carry it to the side of the house. Then they went to admire the new ceremonial fire pit that had been created in the garden while Martha was gone. It was a large sand circle surrounded by boulders for people to sit on. "Let's initiate it," she said. "My first ceremonial fire. To celebrate my new life. I have finally embraced my full power."

"We need something to burn," he said. They both had the same idea at the same moment. Dragging the sign to the center of the fire pit, they kindled a fire around it. Soon it was blazing.

Martha got her cell phone and dialed the agent's number before it disappeared in flames. "I'm calling about your listing at 14 Owl Hill," she said sweetly.

"A beautiful house. I would be happy to show it to you."

"How much are you trying to get for it?" Martha inquired. When the agent mentioned the asking price, Martha was shocked.

"It's immaculate," the agent continued. "And the garden is spectacular. You really need to see it. There are some very unusual plantings and a lovely imported fountain. And there is enough property that the land could be subdivided. I do have an interested party who wants to tear the house down to put in condominiums because of the view."

Martha had heard enough. "This is Martha Peggity. A few moments ago I took the liberty of de-listing the house. There is certainly not going to be a condominium there. Your sign is burning as we speak." As the agent sputtered in disbelief, she hung up.

"I can't believe I gave my power away for so many years," she told Ned. "I never even realized I was doing it. And once I became aware of it, I was afraid to stop. I was afraid people would be mad at me. But I finally realized I can't be wishy-washy. It's what Aurora told me the first day. It just took some time for it to sink in. Force of habit, I guess."

Ned nodded. "You're much more interesting like this. I want to have the same experience."

"You've started," she said. "That's all it takes." She turned to watch the fire. "I never knew I had all this inside me. I always felt there was something more, but I didn't know what it was. The first action I ever took on my own was buying this house, and I think that's what started everything. I wanted to see what it felt like to pursue my own dream, and my dream was to have a house like this. It seems like such a little thing now, but look at what's happened because of it. Look at all the people who came into my life. Look at everything that's come about."

"And because of you, look what's happened to me," Ned said. "I got to fly in a UFO! I never told you, but that's the moment that hooked me."

She smiled. "You know, I have been thinking about a woman I met in England. I'm going to pay her a visit soon. I want to share with her what's happened to me and tell her about the classes. If you want to go along, you could have a chat with her husband."

"Never been to England. Offer accepted. I have a feeling my life is never going to be the same."

"That's the other thing Aurora told me the first day. Little did I know," she said.

Carol arrived to see what was going on. "I couldn't believe your house was for sale," she said. "I was shocked, to tell you the truth. Aren't you supposed to return the sign? I don't imagine the agent will be too happy you burned it."

"Carol," Martha said. "If you could do something that you always wanted do do, what would it be?"

Carol looked at her, not comprehending. "I never thought about it," she said. "Certainly no one's ever asked me about it."

"Think about it," Martha said. "There's no rush."

"I'd take a cruise," Carol said suddenly. "But Joe doesn't want to."

"I'd love to go," Ned said. "Why don't you and I plan something like that? We haven't spent any time together, just the two of us, since I don't know when."

"Well," Carol said, hesitating. "I don't know. What would Joe do by himself?"

"Why don't we ask him," Martha suggested as Joe appeared.

"Wondered what all the smoke was. What's going on?"

"We are talking about our dreams," Martha replied. "If you could do something you would love to do, what would it be?"

Joe thought for a minute, glancing over at Carol as if he were afraid to say. For some reason, he felt empowered. "It's kind of silly," he said, "but I'd like to go fishing for a week with a buddy of mine. I don't like the idea of leaving Carol alone."

"Well," Martha said. "Carol won't be alone. She's going on a cruise with Ned." Joe looked surprised, and Carol just stood there without saying a word.

"I suppose that would be OK," Joe said. "Wow. That's a lot to think about." He started grinning from ear to ear. "Bill and I haven't gone on a fishing trip since I can't remember when. Our wives don't like to fish."

"And our husbands don't like cruises." Carol was grinning now too. "Thank you, Martha. I'm...well, it's good you're not moving."

"Say, whatever happened to your cat?" Joe asked.

"He's doing very well," Martha said. "He's with a friend of mine. Which reminds me, I'm off to see Aurora. Ned, will you keep an eye on things here?"

Martha combed her hair and packed a sandwich, just in case. Adventures, she had learned, were part of the experience. It was good to be ready for whatever happened. She tucked her cell phone in her pocket and stepped into the portal. She felt like a new person, full of energy and ready for anything.

21

S teven greeted Martha warmly when she arrived at the school. "Great work in dreamtime," he said. "I was concerned when I heard you were there, but as it turns out, I didn't need to worry. Our students never cease to amaze us." He pointed in the direction of the office. "Aurora is expecting you. By the way, welcome to the faculty!"

Aurora was in the office studying her computer screen when Martha came in, and Martha waited impatiently for her to look up. "Ah, there you are," Aurora finally said. "You have something on your mind, I see."

"How can I be on the faculty?" she asked, somewhat flustered. "I thought I was a Level 2."

"I see you ran into Steven. Have a seat." When Martha was settled in a chair she continued. "The announcement is a little premature. There's something you must do first." Martha fell silent, feeling a familiar sensation, as if she already knew she wasn't going to understand what Aurora was going to say.

"You are going to be a teacher of the lost arts," Aurora said. "You are going to be someone who empowers people in the way that you have been empowered. But first, there is something you must do."

Martha waited expectantly.

Aurora looked directly at her. "You will visit the Lost City."

"The Lost City," Martha exclaimed.

"Kawak is taking you. There you will have your final training."

"Who?"

"The quetzal you met in the rainforest. He has come to tell me."

"Where is it? How long will I be there?"

"There you go again, firing questions because you're nervous." Aurora waited a moment. "The Lost City is deep in the jungle, accessible by a five-day burro ride over narrow trails through the mountains." Martha looked aghast. "Or by portal. It is your choice." Aurora smiled. "Actually, I am not sure the path is open anymore. There have been many landslides in the area. And the vegetation grows quickly. That first day in the rainforest," she added, "you were very near. Kawak steered you away. You weren't ready yet to go there. We have been waiting until you were. This is why you were given the amulet, because you answered Kawak's call."

Martha stared in disbelief. Just when she thought she knew something, she discovered that there was still a great deal to learn.

"There you will learn the Manipulative Arts. The name is misleading to the novice. These arts teach you the details of creating your life and overcoming apparent obstacles. You will be astounded at what you learn and you will wonder how you could not have seen this on your own. It is amazing, really. You will also learn about accessing the future. It is possible to access a future healed state to bring that healing into the present. It is a gift that will change humanity." Aurora studied her for a moment. "You learn quickly; it won't take you long at all. Once again, you will discover that what you need to know is already inside you. It will move from a dormant state to active status. These skills are simply being reawakened."

"When do I go?"

"As soon as you're ready."

Martha was taken aback by the news, as she had looked forward to spending some time at home. "I know," she said. "Spend a couple of days at home if I want. I hear you thinking."

Aurora smiled at her. "How quickly you learn. Soon you will be teaching me."

Martha surveyed the room that had become so familiar to her. Briefly, she thought about that first day in the rainforest, when she had almost ended up in the Lost City. Fortunately the quetzal steered her to the path. Like Aurora said, she hadn't been ready then. Now she was. She had embraced her true power and her essential being. She was almost ready to teach others who were hungry for this information. She would soon be able to show those who felt powerless the way to their power, through awakening what was dormant within them.

But first she would head home to tell everyone goodbye. She had never felt so incredibly alive. But there was still something she didn't know. "I haven't talked to you about how to use the amulet. What do I do with it?"

"You wear it as the current keeper. In time, everything you need to know will be revealed. Learning about the lost arts is a process. You can't do it overnight. You don't yet have enough power to know everything. But you're learning quickly, perhaps more quickly than anyone I've ever seen. In time, what you need to know will be revealed to you. Trust the process. And—"

"I know. Trust myself."

"I was going to say have fun. It is easy to be serious. It is important to remember to enjoy yourself. Let your sense of fun out. It's contagious. It will serve you well."

Martha nodded. Just when she thought she was getting it, there was something new. It was a lot to hold in her mind. Would she ever be able to do this? Would she ever—she stopped herself, and Aurora smiled.

"We will see you soon," Aurora said, walking her to the same door she had entered just a few short weeks ago. "Sooner than you know. Remember, the flame is lit inside you. And the mystery, which guides you, will never be completely known. Even though it surrounds you, it never completely reveals itself. Just when you think you understand it, it changes. It seems to lead away, yet it leads directly inward, to the heart, and inward further, to the soul, and inward further, back to itself, in the great circle."

They said their good-byes, and Martha headed out to the portal. In the courtyard she encountered a young woman who seemed hesitant. "I'm looking for Aurora," she said.

"You'll find her right in there." Martha pointed to the office she had just left.

"I don't have an appointment," the woman said.

"Don't worry, she's expecting you. You've come at exactly the right moment."